The HOUSE with Chicken Legs

SOPHIE ANDERSON

ILLUSTRATED BY ELISA PAGANELLI

USBORNE

CONTENTS

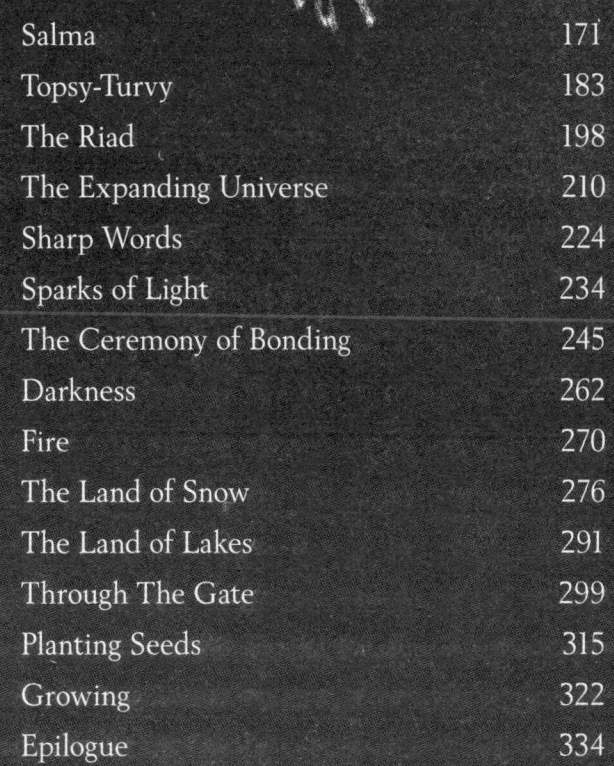

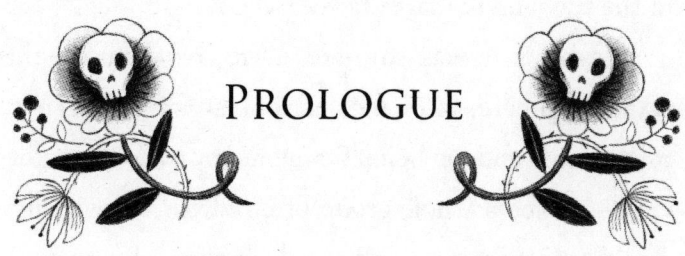

PROLOGUE

My house has chicken legs. Two or three times a year, without warning, it stands up in the middle of the night and walks away from where we've been living. It might walk a hundred miles or it might walk a thousand, but where it lands is always the same. A lonely, bleak place at the edge of civilization.

It nestles in dark forbidden woods, rattles on windswept icy tundra, and hides in crumbling ruins at the far edge of cities. At this moment it's perched on a rocky ledge high in some barren mountains. We've been here two weeks and I still haven't seen anyone living. Dead people, I've seen plenty of those of course. They come to visit Baba and she guides them through

The Gate. But the real, live, living people, they all stay in the town and villages far below us.

Maybe if it was summer a few of them would wander up here, to picnic and look at the view. They might smile and say hello. Someone my own age might visit – maybe a whole group of children. They might stop near the stream and splash in the water to cool off. Perhaps they would invite me to join them.

"How's the fence coming?" Baba calls through the open window, pulling me from my daydream.

"Nearly done." I wedge another thigh bone into the low stone wall. Usually I sink the bones straight into the earth, but up here the ground is too rocky, so I built a knee-high stone wall all the way around the house, pushed the bones into it and balanced the skulls on top. But it keeps collapsing in the night. I don't know if it's the wind, or wild animals, or clumsy dead people, but every day we've been here I've had to rebuild a part of the fence.

Baba says the fence is important to keep out the living and guide in the dead, but that's not why I fix it. I like to work with the bones because my parents would have touched them once, long ago, when they built fences and guided the dead. Sometimes I think I feel the warmth of their hands lingering on the cold bones, and I imagine what it might have been like to hold my parents for real. This makes my heart lift and ache all at the same time.

The house creaks loudly and leans over until the front window is right above me. Baba pokes her head out and smiles. "Lunch is ready. I've made a feast of *shchi* and black bagels. Enough for Jack too."

My stomach rumbles as the smell of cabbage soup and freshly baked bread hits my nose. "Just the gate hinge, then I'm done." I lift up a foot bone, wire it back into place, and look around for Jack.

He's picking at a weathered piece of rock underneath a dried-up heather bush, probably hoping to find a woodlouse or a beetle. "Jack!" I call and he tilts his head up. One of his silver eyes flashes as it catches the light. He bounds towards me in an ungainly cross between flying and jumping, lands on my shoulder, and tries to push something into my ear.

"Get off!" My hand darts up to cover my ear. Jack's always stashing food to save for later. I don't know why he thinks my ears are a good hiding place. He forces the thing into my fingers instead; something small, dry and crispy. I pull my hand down to look. It's a crumpled, broken spider. "Thanks, Jack." I drop the carcass into my pocket. I know he means well, sharing his food, but I've had enough of dead things. "Come on." I shake my head and sigh. "Baba's made a feast. For two people and a jackdaw."

I turn and look at the town far below us. All those houses, snuggled close together, keeping each other company in this cold and lonely place. I wish my house was a normal house, down there, with the living. I wish my family was a normal family, too. But my house has chicken legs, and my grandmother is a Yaga and a Guardian of The Gate between this world and the next. So my wishes are as hollow as the skulls of the fence.

GUIDING
THE DEAD

I light the candles in the skulls at dusk. An orange glow flickers out from their empty eye sockets, beckoning the dead. They appear on the horizon like mist and take shape as they stumble over the rocky ground towards the house.

When I was younger I used to try to guess what their lives had been like, or what pets they might have had, but now I'm twelve years old I'm bored of that game. My gaze is drawn to the lights of the town glistening far below; a universe of possibilities.

I jump as Jack swoops out of the darkness and lands on the window sill next to me. His claws click against the wood and he ruffles his feathers. It sounds like the wind in the trees and I think of the freedom in the air.

"I wish I could fly down there, Jack." I stroke the back of his neck. "And spend an evening with the living." I think of all the things the living might be doing, things I've only read about in books but could actually do if I went to the town: run races or play games with other children; watch a show in a theatre surrounded by warm, smiling faces…

"Marinka!" Baba calls and the window blinks shut.

"Coming, Baba." I throw on my headscarf and run to the door. I should be there to greet the dead with her, to watch as she guides them through The Gate. After all, it's "a serious responsibility" and I have to "focus" and "learn the ways" so I can do it on my own one day. I don't want to think about that day. Baba says it's my destiny to become the next Guardian and, when I do, my first duty will be to guide her through The Gate. A shudder bursts through my chest and I shake it off. Like I said, I don't want to think about that day.

Baba is stirring a great cauldron of *borsch* over a roaring fire. She turns and smiles as I enter the room, an excited twinkle in her eyes. "You look lovely, my *pchelka*. Are you ready?"

I nod and force a smile, wishing I loved guiding as much as she does.

"Look." Baba glances at her chair where a violin sits, freshly strung and polished. "I finally got round to mending it. I hope one of the dead will play us some fresh tunes."

"That would be nice." The prospect of new music would have excited me not so long ago, but these days, no matter which of her old musical instruments Baba fixes up, the nights spent guiding all feel the same. "Shall I pour the *kvass*?" I look at the table, where an army of stout glasses are waiting to be filled with the dark, pungent drink.

"Yes, please." Baba nods. I push my way through the steamy sour smells as she wails a song off-key, swaying a spoonful of the bright red beetroot soup up to her lips. "More garlic," she mutters and throws a handful of raw cloves into the mix.

I open a bottle and pour the *kvass*. Its yeasty stench plumes into the air, mixing effortlessly with the reek of the soup. I watch the creamy coloured bubbles rise through the dark brown liquid and erupt into a thick, foamy froth on the surface. One by one the bubbles pop and disappear just like the dead will all vanish at the end of the night. It seems so pointless getting to know the dead when we'll never see them again. But it's our duty as Yaga, living in this Yaga house, to talk to them and give them one last wonderful evening reliving their memories and celebrating their lives, before they pass through The Gate and return to the stars.

"They're here!" Baba exclaims and she sweeps across the room, arms outstretched. An old man is hovering in the doorway. He's faint and wispy, a sure sign he's been expecting this for some time. It won't take long for him to pass through The Gate.

Baba talks to him softly in the language of the dead, as I fill the table. Bowls and spoons, thick black bread, a basket of dill, pots of sour cream and horseradish, mushroom dumplings, an assortment of tiny glasses and a large bottle of spirit *trost* – the fiery drink for the dead. Baba says it's named *trost* after a walking stick because it helps the dead on their journey.

I try to listen to them, try to focus and understand what they're saying, but the language of the dead evades me. I've always found it more difficult than the languages of the living, which I pick up as easily as shells on a beach.

My mind keeps drifting to the town. The way it curves around the narrow end of the lake. I've seen the living go out on little fishing boats in the morning, in groups of two or three. I wonder what it would be like to row one with a friend. We could go all the way to the island in the middle and explore it together. Maybe build a fire and camp under the stars...

Baba nudges me gently as she helps the old man into a chair. "Would you get a bowl of *borsch* for our guest, please?"

More dead flood in. Daydreams loiter at the edge of my mind as I serve, arrange chairs and bring cushions, and try to reassure the dead with smiles and nods. Soon they relax, warmed by food and drink and the lick and crackle of flames in the hearth. The house gives them energy and they become more solid, until they almost seem alive. Almost.

Laughter echoes around the rafters and the house murmurs with satisfaction as the dead reminisce about their prides and joys, and sigh at their sorrows and regrets. The house lives for the dead. Baba too. She flits from guest to guest, her twisted old body now nimble as a hummingbird.

On the few occasions the living have wandered close to the house, I've heard their whispers. I've heard them call Baba ugly, hideous, a witch, or a monster. I've heard them say she eats people. But they've never seen her like this. She's beautiful, dancing among the dead, bringing comfort and joy. I love her wide, crooked-toothed smile, her big warty nose, and her thinning white hair that floats out from under her skulls-and-flowers headscarf. I love her comfortable, fat belly and her bowed, stumpy legs. I love her ability to make everyone feel at ease. The dead come here lost and confused, but they leave calm and peaceful and ready for their journey.

Baba is a perfect Guardian. Far better than I will ever be. But then, I don't want to be a Guardian. Being a Guardian means being responsible for The Gate and all the guiding of the dead, for ever. And while guiding makes Baba happy, seeing the dead drift away every night makes me feel even more alone. If only I was destined to be something else. Something that involved living people.

The house shifts its weight, settling into the night, and opens its skylights wide. Stars twinkle above us, raining down tiny sparks of light. *"Trost!"* Baba shouts and she pulls the cork out of the bottle with her teeth. The sweet, spicy smell of the drink fills the air and the fire burns brighter.

The Gate appears in the corner of the room, near the hearth. It's a large black rectangle. Blacker than the darkness at the bottom of a grave. It draws your gaze like a black hole draws light, and the longer you stare at it, the stronger it pulls you in.

I move towards it, hands in my apron pocket, avoiding its yawn by looking at the floor. The floorboards seem to flow into the chasm and disappear into the blackness. Out of the corners of my eyes, I see fleeting glimpses of light and colour deep inside the void. The sweep of a rainbow, the twinkle of nebulae, billowing storm clouds, and the infinite arc of the Milky Way. An ocean breathes far below and water smashes against the glassy mountains. I scoop the dead spider from my pocket and place it on the floor.

The spider's soul pulls itself out of the carcass and looks around the room in confusion. Animals don't need to be guided – Baba says they understand the great cycle better than humans – so it's probably wondering why it's in a Yaga house.

I mumble the death journey words anyway, forgetting half of them and mispronouncing the rest. Something about strength on the long and arduous path, gratitude for time on Earth, and peace at returning to the stars. The dead spider tilts its head at me and looks even more confused. I sigh and brush it into The Gate, wondering for the millionth time if destinies are fixed. If I really do have to become a Guardian and spend my life saying goodbyes, when I ache to have friendships that last for more than one night.

Baba starts singing and the dead join her. Their voices rise higher and louder. One of them picks up the violin and plays, faster and faster. Baba gets her accordion and the music swells. The house bounces in time to the beat and the dead stamp their feet and spin and dance. But slowly, one by one, they tire and sigh and drift towards The Gate. Baba puts down her accordion. She whispers the death journey words into the ears of the dead, kisses their cheeks, and they sink into the darkness, smiling as they float away.

When the first light of dawn dims the stars above, there is only one left. A young girl, wrapped in one of Baba's black-and-red shawls, staring into the fire. The young always find it hardest to pass through The Gate. It seems unfair that their time spent on Earth is so short. Baba says "it's not how long a life, but how sweet a life that counts". She says some souls learn what they've come here to learn quickly and others take their time. I don't see why we can't all have long, sweet lives, lessons aside.

Baba gives the child sugared almonds, holds her close, and whispers in her ear words I don't understand, and eventually the girl nods and lets Baba guide her through The Gate. As the girl drifts away, pale golden rays of sunlight fall through the skylights and The Gate disappears. The skylights blink shut and the house sighs. Baba dabs a tear from the corner of her eye, although when she turns to me she's smiling, so I'm not sure if she is happy or sad. "Cocoa?" she asks, her mind still stuck in the language of the dead.

"Yes, please." I nod and begin to clear away the dishes.

"Did you listen to the astronomer who had a star named after her?" Baba's face lights up, as she reverts to our usual chatter. "I guided a stargazer to the stars!"

I try to picture all the faces of the dead and work out who she might have been, but I have no idea. "I still find the language of the dead really difficult."

"You understood it when I offered you cocoa."

"That's different." Blood rushes into my cheeks. "Cocoa is just one word. The dead all talk too fast."

Baba passes me my mug, filled to the brim with the hot sweet drink, and sits in her chair by the fire. "What shall we read this morning?"

I slide my headscarf off, sit on my floor cushion, and lean against Baba's knees. She always reads to me before we go to bed for our morning sleep. "Will you tell me a story about my parents instead?" I ask.

Baba strokes my hair. "Which one would you like to hear?"

"How they met."

"Again?" she asks.

"Again." I nod.

"Well." Baba takes a sip of cocoa. "You know both your parents were from ancient Yaga families, with ancestors stretching all the way back to the First Yaga of The Steppes."

Jack carefully folds a piece of honey bread into the fabric of my skirt and I stroke the soft feathers on the side of his face.

"Your mother's house had been galloping from The Great Mountains in the East, and your father's house from The Jagged Peaks in the West. Without warning, both houses suddenly turned south and settled on the outskirts of The Sinking City for the night, to soak their legs in the water."

"The houses' feet were so hot from running..." I prompt.

"The water sizzled and steamed in the moonlight." Baba smiles. "Your mother looked out of her window and was so taken with the beauty of the city that she snuck out and borrowed a gondola, so she could explore the canals in the quiet of the night."

I imagine my mother floating over a smooth, dark, reflected sky, which gently sloshes against her boat as she strokes her oar through the starry waters.

"Not far away" – Baba taps her foot on the floor rhythmically – "your father, also taken with the beauty of the city, was dancing on the roof of his house."

I laugh. "He still lived with his parents?"

Baba nods. "Your mother had been living in a Yaga house of her own for a few years, but your father still lived with his Yaga parents."

"My father saw my mother, leaned over for a closer look…" I wait for Baba to finish my sentence.

She leans over me, like my father leaning over on the roof of his house. "Your father tripped and plummeted." Baba's eyes widen in mock fear. "Down and down, towards the canal...and then he landed, hard, in your mother's boat. It rocked so much your mother fell into the water, screaming."

"My father dived in to save her," I rush in. "But he tripped again as he jumped out of the gondola, banged his head, and ended up unconscious in the canal."

Baba rests her hand on my shoulder. "And so your mother ended up saving him."

"Then they fell in love, and had me." I smile.

"Well that was a few years later. But yes, they had you. You were their world, Marinka. They loved you so much."

I sigh and put my empty mug down. I love that story – not because of the moonlit canals, or the

dancing on the roof, or the falling into the water and being saved, although they are all good bits. I love that story because although my mother broke the Yaga rules, sneaking out of the house and stealing a gondola in the middle of the night, nothing bad happened because of it. And I love the idea that one day, completely out of the blue, someone or something could come hurtling down from the sky and change my life, for ever.

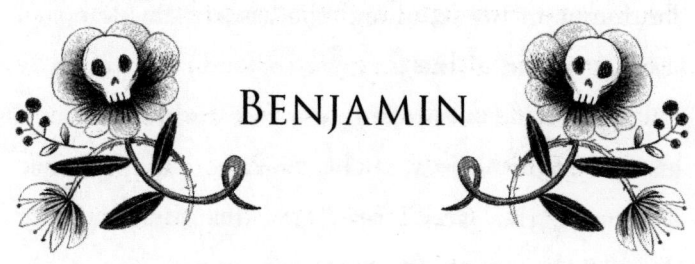

BENJAMIN

Jack stands on the wall, his grey-black feathers ruffling in the breeze as he watches me struggle to squeeze a thigh bone back into place. The sun is high in the sky but the air is still cold. Only a small part of the fence collapsed last night, but my hands are frozen, so it's taking longer than it should to fix.

"*Caaaaaw!*" Jack shouts an alarm call right next to my ear that makes me wince as I turn around. A boy, about my age, is standing just a few paces away. I blink, wondering if my daydreams are becoming more real as well as more frequent. But he doesn't disappear. My heart races with excitement. He's a real, live, living boy. His long, dark coat is open and a tiny winter lamb is poking its nose out from beneath his armpit.

"Umm, are they human bones?" The boy looks at the femur in my hand and the assortment of bones sticking up out of the wall.

"Yes. No." I scramble to my feet and try to block his view of the nearest, obviously human, skull. "What I mean is, they aren't real." The lie catches in my throat and I feel my face reddening.

"They look real." A smile plays at the corner of his mouth. He doesn't seem scared, just curious.

"Well, I suppose they are real." I rest the femur on top of the wall, my fingers trembling. I don't want to scare him away. "What I mean is, they aren't fresh."

He raises his eyebrows.

"Like, I didn't kill anyone."

"Oh, I didn't think you did." He looks along the wall, then beyond it to the house. It's sitting low, legs folded underneath it, so it looks fairly normal, like a small log cabin. "Are you on holiday or something?"

"I just moved here, with my grandmother."

"I've never noticed this house here before. Where did it come from?"

"It walked here."

Baba would scold me for telling the truth, but I learned a long time ago that nobody believes me when I say the house walks anyway, and it's easier than making up even more ridiculous lies. The boy looks from the house to me, and smiles politely. He thinks I'm joking and he's waiting for the real explanation.

"I'm Marinka." I hold out my hand, eager to change the subject and touch a real, live, living person (I suppose technically Baba is alive, but she doesn't count, what with her being so old).

The boy takes my hand in his. It's warm and slightly damp with sweat. A smile bursts across my face and my cheeks ache with the force of it. I can't remember the last time I spoke to a living person, let alone touched one. It must be at least a year ago. Even longer since it was someone my own age.

"I'm Benjamin." He pulls his hand away and I wonder for a moment if I gripped it too tight, but then I'm distracted by the lamb wriggling under his coat.

"Can I stroke it?" I ask. Benjamin nods and I gently ruffle the top of the lamb's head. "It's tiny."

"He's only a few days old. An orphan. I'm taking him home to hand-rear."

"How wonderful. I'd love a lamb."

Benjamin looks at Jack cautiously. He's strutting back and forth along the wall, his eyes firmly locked on the lamb.

"Oh, Jack wouldn't hurt him," I say, wondering, just for a moment, if he would.

"Is he your pet?"

"Sort of." I lift my elbow and Jack hops onto it. "I raised him from a chick. He was an orphan too. I found him on The Island of Standing Stones."

"Did your house walk there too?" Benjamin smiles and his eyes shine with mischief.

"The house can't walk on water! It swam there." I laugh nervously as it occurs to me how ridiculous that must sound to him.

Benjamin tucks the lamb deeper into his coat and glances up at the sky. A cold wave of panic crashes over me, because he's about to leave and I'll be alone again. This could be my last chance to talk to a living person for, well, maybe years.

"Would you like some *kvass*?" I ask quickly.

"What's that?"

"A drink." I bite my lip, wishing I'd offered him something else. We're far away from The Steppes, in a place that Baba calls The Land of Lakes. Of course Benjamin won't know what *kvass* is. And it would probably taste really strange to him. The lamb bleats, incredibly powerfully for such a little thing. "Something for the lamb!" I exclaim far too loudly as the idea hits me.

"Ummm. I should..." Benjamin looks at the house suspiciously and I wonder if it woke up and did something to scare him, like shift its weight or poke out a claw. I glance back and am relieved to see it's still asleep.

"Please." My chest aches from wanting and willing him to stay. "I haven't met anyone from round here yet," I say, "and I'd like to learn about the town and..." My voice trails away as I look into Benjamin's eyes. They're big, brown and friendly, and my heart does a little flip as I realize he is going to stay.

"All right." He smiles. "I'll try some *kvass*, and if

you bring some warm water out I've got something to feed the lamb."

I tread softly, so as not to wake the house. We used to play a game when I was little called Yaga's Footsteps, in which I would try to sneak up on the house and touch its legs before it heard me and chased me away. Because of that game I know all the house's blind and deaf spots, and all the places I can sit and watch for the living without it ever knowing.

Baba is asleep in her chair by the fire. I decide cocoa will be more familiar to Benjamin, and take longer to drink than *kvass*. So I silently lift three mugs from the shelf above the hearth, scoop cocoa, milk powder and sugar into two of them and carefully pour warm water from the kettle hanging over the fire into all three.

Jack lands on the porch with a thud and his claws click across the wooden floor towards me. I shoot him an angry look and lift my finger to my lips. He stops, tilts his head and shrugs his wings in a nonchalant apology. As I creep out with the mugs he follows me, his claws tapping even louder than before. Honestly, sometimes I think he wants me to get into trouble.

Benjamin is sitting on a large rock overlooking the valley, just the other side of the fence. It's big enough for both of us and another flutter of excitement runs through me because in a moment I will be sitting next to a real, live, living person.

Maybe we'll talk and become friends. Maybe he'll visit me again, and we'll go for walks and play games, like other children do – or at least, I think they do. My heart feels like it might burst at the thought and the mugs tremble in my hands.

The bone-gate would rattle and wake the house, so I step over the wall where the fence has fallen. A cool gust of wind takes my breath away. I'm not supposed to go further than the fence, but every time I do, even though it's never for more than a few paces, I feel more alive. Everything seems bigger, brighter and more colourful, and I wonder if this is how my mother felt when she went out in the middle of the night and stole the gondola.

"This smells like cocoa," Benjamin says after sniffing his drink.

"Oh, it is cocoa."

"I thought we were having *kvass*?"

"This is warmer than *kvass*." I take a sip of mine and buzz as the warmth and sugar flow down into my belly.

Benjamin balances his mug on the edge of the rock and pulls a bottle and a crumpled envelope out of his pocket.

"Is that for the lamb?" I ask.

"Yes. It's a special kind of milk powder." He pours some into the bottle, covers it with warm water,

shakes it up, and then swaps the bottle top for one with a teat on it. "Would you like to feed him?"

"Oh, yes please." I put my mug down and Benjamin lifts the lamb onto my lap. I try to wrap my shawl around him but it's difficult because his thin legs keep kicking clumsily around. Eventually he settles into an uncomfortable-looking position and Benjamin passes the bottle over.

The lamb sucks greedily, milk dripping out of one side of his mouth. Jack squawks theatrically and struts off to the withered heather bush, where he makes a show of flipping over stones to look for bugs. He's jealous. I'll make it up to him later; give him something nice from the pantry.

Benjamin watches the lamb for a while, then picks up his mug again. "So will you go to the school in town?"

I shake my head. "I'm homeschooled, because we move around so much." I don't tell him it's because I have to learn how to be the next Guardian; that I have to learn the language of the dead and the death journey words, how to cook for the dead and guide them through The Gate. Baba says the living aren't supposed to know these things, and I'd rather talk about his life anyway. "Do you go to school?" I ask, wondering what it would be like to sit in a room filled with children and play games with them during breaks. Just imagining it makes me feel giddy.

"Usually. I've been suspended though."

"What does that mean?"

"I'm not allowed to go for a week. It's not because I'm bad or anything," Benjamin adds quickly. "It was because of a stupid argument with some boys that got out of hand. None of us meant it to." Benjamin sighs. "I just don't fit in there, you know?"

I nod, but I don't know. I've never had the chance to see if I fit in or not.

"How come you move around so much?" he asks.

"My grandmother is a musician. She likes to travel, for inspiration." I pass the empty bottle back to Benjamin, but keep the lamb on my lap. He's so warm. There is nothing like the warmth of the living; it seems to soak deep into my soul.

"What about your parents?" Benjamin swigs the last of his cocoa.

"My parents died when I was a baby." The image of a Yaga house desperately trying to outrun the flames engulfing it burns through my mind. I blink it away and take a slow breath in, trying to ease the cramping in my chest.

"My mother died when I was a baby too," Benjamin says quietly.

A ripple of understanding relaxes the muscles around my ribs. It feels nice to have something in common with Benjamin, even if it is something as awful as this.

"I think about my mother all the time." Benjamin carefully wraps the lamb's bottle up in waxed paper. "Even though I never knew her."

"I know what you mean." I nod. "I wonder what my life would be like if my parents had lived." My chest tightens again as I think of my gondola-stealing mother and my roof-dancing father. Would they have understood why I don't want to be a Guardian? Would they have let me be something else? I turn to Benjamin, willing him to change the subject.

"So it's just you, your grandmother, your jackdaw,

and your walking house." Benjamin lifts his eyebrows and smiles.

"Yep." I nod. "And we move around a lot. And I don't go to school. So it can get pretty lonely." I laugh, although it's not funny at all.

"Well, it can be lonely at school too, even when you're surrounded by people."

"How can you be lonely surrounded by people?"

"You know, if they aren't friendly, or if they don't understand you."

I think about all my nights guiding the dead – how I can be surrounded by them but still feel alone. I always thought it was because they're dead and I'm alive. I didn't realize you could feel like that among the living.

"So what's with the bones in your wall?" Benjamin asks.

"It's kind of a tradition."

"Like Hallowe'en or something?"

"Something like that." I look down to the town by the lake, and the little villages surrounding it. "Do you live in the town?"

"I live in that village, there." Benjamin leans close and points across the valley. I feel the warmth of his breath against my cheek and I stop still, my whole body tingling. He leans back and points in the other direction, along the mountain. "I've been helping out at a farm over there, in the next valley. It was my father's idea. He wants to keep me busy while I'm suspended. That's where I got the lamb from." Benjamin nods at the lamb, now asleep in my lap. "I'm a bit worried my father won't let me keep him, to be honest."

"Oh, I'm sure he will. How could he resist?" I stroke the soft downy fur under the lamb's chin.

"You're probably right." Benjamin nods slowly. "But I should have asked him first. He's not too happy with me, you know, over the suspension thing." He pauses and his eyes widen. "Hey, I've got an idea. Why don't you keep the lamb, just until tomorrow? I'll ask my father tonight, then come back and pick him up in the morning? Would you mind?"

"I...I..." My head spins. Of course I want to keep the lamb and see Benjamin again in the morning.

I've dreamed about making a friend for as long as I can remember. A living, human friend my own age; to talk to and do things with. And Benjamin and I have so much in common. It's like this is meant to be! But what about the house? And Baba? If they find out I've been talking to a living soul, they won't let me out of their sight for a month. Probably longer. I look at Benjamin and his big easy smile melts all my worries away. "I'd love to have him," I say.

But the moment Benjamin has walked away and I step back over the wall, my worries crowd around me, a hundred times darker and heavier than before... because the house has sat up on its haunches and is staring right at me, a deep frown on its two front windows.

A
TOO-HEAVY
BLANKET

"We can fatten him up and make lamb *borsch* in the spring." Baba grins.

"No!" I pull the lamb tight against my body and try to cover him with my shawl.

"Well, what are you going to do with him then? He'll grow into a fat, hungry sheep, and the house doesn't always settle on grassland."

"I won't keep him long. Just until he's strong enough to be outside on his own." I glance out of the window. I've decided when Benjamin picks the lamb up tomorrow, I'll tell Baba he ran off.

The floorboards roll beneath me and I stumble forwards.

Baba raises her eyebrows. "Where exactly did you find him?"

"I told you already. He was near the fence, alone and abandoned." I look down at the lamb, my cheeks burning.

"Which side of the fence?"

The chimney sighs loudly. I know the house saw me stepping back over the wall, but I'm still hoping it didn't see me with Benjamin. "I'm not really sure." I bite my lip and look at the rafters. "It was hard to tell because the fence had collapsed. I was fixing it and I heard him bleating."

Baba shakes her head and frowns. "You know you shouldn't go beyond the fence. It's not safe—"

"I didn't go far," I interrupt. "What was I supposed to do? Leave him there all alone?"

"You could have told me. I would have come with you."

"You were asleep and I didn't want to wake you. Honestly, he was barely the other side of the fence." I look straight into her eyes, because that bit of the story is true.

Baba's face relaxes a little. "All right. Just promise me—"

"I won't do it again, I promise." I flash my most dazzling smile. "So can I keep him?"

Baba gives a little nod and smiles back. "You can use some of the bones to build him a shelter on the porch."

"Thank you!" I run out of the back door and along the wrap-around porch until I come to the smooth, wide floorboards near the water butt. This is one of the house's deaf spots, so it won't hear me if I talk to the lamb.

I tuck the lamb up in my shawl, place him in a large empty bucket, and spend the rest of the day building him the finest shelter I can. As I wire the bones into place I examine them carefully, wondering which ones were from my parents' house. Baba said all that was left after the fire was the bones from their fence, so she brought them here and they've become jumbled up with ours. I wish I had something else of my parents, something other than bones to remember them by.

Dusk dims the sky and Jack shouts from the top of a skull at the far end of the fence. It's time to light the candles already. I feed the lamb first, and fill his shelter with old woollen blankets so he's nice and warm. Then I light the candles in the skulls and open the bone-gate ready for the arrival of the dead.

The evening carries me along in a daze. I'm even more distracted than usual. I drop bowls, knock over chairs, and jump at every noise from outside. Baba thinks it's because I'm worried about the lamb, which I am, but mostly I'm thinking about the morning and Benjamin returning. Butterflies are battering my insides with excitement and panic.

After I smash the second glass of the evening, Baba suggests I get the lamb and take him to my bedroom. She drops a whiskery kiss onto my cheek and tells me to get some sleep, but I know I won't be able to. I'm far too charged up about tomorrow.

I push open my bedroom door and a smile creeps across my face. The house has grown a small shelter for the lamb in the corner of my room, complete with a grassy floor and miniature fence. Right next to it is a mossy fort, like the ones it used to grow for me to play in when I was little.

The trouble is, I'm not little any more. Looking at the fort, an uncomfortable feeling settles over me, like a too-heavy blanket. Playing make-believe games with the house was exciting when I was young. The house would grow me cosy dens and miniature worlds, tiny walking trees and dancing flowers. Happiness would swell inside me and I felt like I might burst.

But now I'm older, no matter what the house grows for me, I still want to leave and explore the real world, meet the living, and have friendships that last for more than one night.

I try to distract myself by reading, but the characters in the story are walking by a lake so I end up imagining what it might be like to go for a walk with Benjamin. I play my word game instead, using the wooden tiles to spell out words like *friend* and *life*, but there is space on the board for another player, so I end up wondering whether Benjamin knows how to play. I give up and sit by the window, staring at the constellations of street lights in the town far below.

The sounds of the guiding swell and fade. Then I hear Baba tuning her *balalaika*. She plays my favourite lullaby from when I was little. But tonight, just like the mossy fort, it makes me feel cramped and restless. I'm relieved when Baba shuffles off to bed and I can return to my daydreams.

The first light of dawn blushes the sky pink and slowly the house begins to relax. When I'm sure it's fast asleep, I pull my shawl tight around my shoulders and silently slip out of the door.

Jack watches from a skull as I pad softly down to the fence. I put my finger to my lips and shoot him a look that I hope says *please don't give me away*. Thankfully it works, although my heart is thumping so loud I think it may wake the house all on its own, and the promise I made to Baba is ringing in my ears.

A freezing mist has gathered around the bones of the fence, coating them with a thin layer of shining ice crystals. I shiver as I look around to check I'm in one of the house's blind spots. Satisfied it can't see me, I step over the fence and settle down on the rock Benjamin and I sat on yesterday, and I wait.

Jack comes and sits next to me, every so often tucking his head under my arm to get a stroke. I feed him pieces of spiced honey bread from my apron pocket and watch the mist slowly clear.

"*Cawww!*" Jack shouts loudly, knocking a skull off the fence as he flaps awkwardly into the air.

My heart jumps into my throat and I turn around to check he didn't wake the house. But it's still asleep, legs folded neatly underneath the porch. I slide off the rock to pick up the skull and when I straighten up I see him. Benjamin. A huge smile warms my cheeks and I wave excitedly.

"Hello." He smiles back. "Still playing with your bones?"

I blush as I realize I have the skull in my hand. "Oh, yes, sorry, it just fell off the fence and—"

"Can I hold it?" Benjamin asks. I pass it to him and he lifts it up to his face and stares into the empty eye sockets. "It's strange, isn't it?"

"What?"

"You know, that this was a living person once, walking around. I wonder what they were like, what kind of life they had."

"Well, whoever it was, they're gone now." I take the skull from him and balance it back on the fence. I spend every night listening to the dead rattle on about what kind of lives they've had. Right now, I want to do some living of my own.

"How's the lamb?" Benjamin asks.

"He's fine. Asleep in my room. I could get him now if you like, but I was hoping maybe we could—" The words freeze on my lips. Last night it had seemed like such a good idea to invite Benjamin to come for a walk, but now doubts are crowding around me. I've never been more than a few steps away from the fence. What if Baba is right? What if it's dangerous out there?

"Go for a walk?" Benjamin finishes my sentence. "I was going to ask you the same thing. I've got to restock a bothy." He points along the mountain. "It's not far away. Would you like to come?"

Still unable to speak, or even breathe, I nod my head and clench my fingers to try and stop them from trembling. I've no idea what a bothy is, or what restocking one involves, but for the first time in my life I'm going to walk away from the house and have an adventure of my own. Dizzy with excitement and anticipation, I take a deep breath, imagine my mother on her stolen gondola, and tell myself this is going to work out fine.

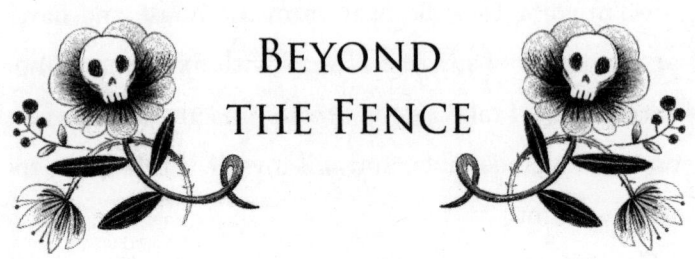

BEYOND
THE FENCE

Once the house disappears from view, I relax. The thought that I might get into trouble is still there, but I've decided it's all the more reason to enjoy every moment while I can.

"What's a bothy?" I finally ask.

"A shelter for walkers. Usually they're little huts, left open for anyone to use, but the one we're going to is a cave in the side of the mountain."

"Why are you restocking it?"

"My father is a teacher. He's bringing some children up here tomorrow on a field trip, so he asked me to drop off some supplies." Benjamin turns to me and smiles. "It's just another excuse to keep me busy really."

"Does he teach at your school?"

"Yes. That's one of the reasons I don't fit in there."

"Really? Why?"

Benjamin shrugs. "Some of the children don't want to be friends with a teacher's son."

My eyebrows knit together. There are so many things I don't understand about the living. Jack flaps out of the mist and I suddenly feel very glad he's with me. "What are the other reasons you don't fit in?" I ask.

"Most of the boys spend all their time talking about, or playing, football."

"And you don't like football?" I glance up and the view takes my breath away. We're crossing a boulder field so deep in mist it looks like the rocks are floating on a cloud.

"No. Not really. I like drawing." Benjamin hops from one rock to the next and his footfalls echo with a strange, sonorous clinking. "They call this place Hollow Stones," he says, "because of the noises the rocks make when you walk over them."

I jump onto a wobbly boulder and shift my weight

back and forth. It's like music. I can't believe this place is so close to the house and I might never have come here. The sounds bounce around inside me as I wonder what else I've missed out on because I'm not supposed to go beyond the fence. The thought makes me feel hollow, like the stones.

Benjamin reaches back and offers me a hand. I could jump the gap to the next boulder easily, but I wrap my fingers around his and beam as he pulls me next to him. "What do you like to draw?" I ask.

"Birds mostly." He looks down and I notice his ears have turned pink. "I guess that's another reason I don't fit in. There aren't many twelve-year-old birdwatchers at school. Sometimes I get teased about it."

"Well, I love birds." I hold my arm out and Jack swoops down, landing on it heavily.

Benjamin looks up and smiles. "He's brilliant."

"Yes." I nod. "He is."

The boulder field ends abruptly. We step onto a gravelly slope and walk slowly up the hill. I can see the cave mouth now, a low, wide scar in the cliff ahead. It's a bit of a scramble climbing up to it, and by the time we reach the cave my legs are aching and my hands feel weird; all cold and numb from pulling myself up on the icy rocks. But as I stand next to Benjamin and look at the view, unbarred by a skeleton fence, I feel incredible. Like I could do anything.

"Shall I make a fire?" Benjamin suggests, lifting his rucksack from his shoulders. "There'll be some tea in here."

"I can do that," I offer. "I build fires at home all the time."

The cave smells of damp, sweaty socks, but I don't care. It feels so good to be somewhere real, live, living people go, and to be here with a real, live, living person. I bounce to the back corner, which is filled with interesting things. Someone has built a low wooden platform, I guess to sit or lie down on, and a small log burner is nestled nearby, with a chimney pushing its way up through the rocks. Logs are stacked neatly beside it, and a few saucepans and enamel bowls are balanced on a rock.

Building the fire is easy; kindling is already prepared, sticks are already cut, and the logs are dry.

In only a few minutes, flames are dancing in the burner and warmth is sweeping through the cave.

"Good fire." Benjamin warms his hands and I smile.

"What will they do on the field trip tomorrow?" I try to imagine what lessons you could have up a mountain, and what it would be like to come up here with a whole group of children. It must be so much fun.

"I think they are studying the rocks." Benjamin lifts a folder out of his rucksack and passes it to me. "All my father's worksheets are in there." He pulls out an assortment of other things – tape measures, balls of string and tiny magnifying glasses – and stacks them all neatly into a box in the corner.

I flick through the papers as Benjamin makes tea but they don't make much sense. I wish I could come up here tomorrow and see for myself what the children will be doing.

"Sandwich?" Benjamin unwraps a small parcel and offers it to me. The bread is perfectly white and square, not like Baba's home-made bread at all.

Benjamin shows me how to stuff my sandwich with thin crispy potatoes so it crunches when I squash it. "Good, isn't it?"

"Mmm." I nod, breaking a crust off for Jack.

"Does he follow you everywhere?"

"Pretty much." I stroke the soft feathers on Jack's chest and give him another piece of bread. He tucks it into my sock and tugs on my bootlaces. "He's always hiding food for later," I explain. "I think it must be an instinct. He shares food too, and he loves to play. He likes rolling and sliding, and swinging on branches. Sometimes I make puzzles for him using sticks and bits of string." Thinking on this makes my heart ache. I love playing with Jack, and when I was younger I used to love playing with the house too, but I've always wanted to play games with a real person. Someone my own age. Baba can be fun, but she is too full of aching bones to run races or play ball games.

"I'm going to draw him." Benjamin pulls a tin of pencils and a thick sketch pad from his rucksack.

"Can I see your pictures?" I ask, leaning over to look at the doodles on the cover.

Benjamin's ears turn pink again but he passes his sketch pad over. It's full of drawings of birds, wildlife and farm animals, all in perfect detail. "These are amazing." I turn a page and find a half-finished portrait of a woman with long straight hair and friendly eyes like his.

"That's my mother." He reaches for the pad. "I've been drawing her from a photograph." He turns the page and takes a pencil from his tin. "Can I sketch you too? I don't get the chance to practise drawing people very often."

I'm not sure where to look, so I carry on feeding Jack pieces of bread as Benjamin's pencil whispers across the paper. He tells me how he wants to study art, and be an artist when he grows up. I wish I could choose what I want to be when I grow up. I wish it so much it hurts, deep inside my chest.

"Do you believe in destiny?" I blurt out.

"I don't know. Do you?"

I look up, out of the cave, and take a deep breath. All my life I've been told I have a destiny. I want to believe that I can escape it, or change it somehow.

But I don't know how to explain that to Benjamin.

I'm still deciding how to answer when Benjamin puts down his pencil, looks from me to the paper, then passes me the pad. I stare at the girl on the page: curly hair and a freckled nose, smiling as she feeds crumbs to a proud jackdaw on the floor. It's strange, seeing myself through someone else's eyes. It makes me feel more real somehow.

"You've captured Jack perfectly and…" I look at my eyes in the picture. Although I'm smiling, my eyes appear sad. Maybe Benjamin meant to draw them like that, maybe not, but either way I think he has captured me perfectly too. "You draw brilliantly."

"Thank you." Benjamin slides the sketch pad back into his rucksack. "I'll do some more work on it tonight then you can have it, if you like. Do you fancy coming into town with me tomorrow? I could show you around."

My heart stops. I want that more than anything; to go to the little town by the lake. But how can I?

Anger burns through me. It's not fair, the house and Baba making me stay inside the fence. What could possibly be so bad about a trip into town with a friend?

"Yes," I say firmly. "I'll come." I'm not sure how, but I will. Because if I let this opportunity to experience friendship and life beyond the fence slip away, I think my heart will shatter into a thousand pieces.

The air is cold as we walk back across Hollow Stones, but my skin feels hot and itchy. My mind is whirring with ideas for escape that fall apart the moment I try to grasp them.

Benjamin stays with me until the house is in sight. It's in the same position as when I left, and it still looks asleep. A smile twitches at the corner of my mouth with the thought that I might have got away without being missed.

We agree to meet the next day. Benjamin tells me he hasn't asked his father about the lamb yet, so I tell him I'm happy to keep him for another night. As I creep back inside the fence everything seems perfect. I think of my mother on her midnight gondola, and how breaking the rules can lead to wonderful things. Today was fantastic, and tomorrow is going to be even better.

Warmth hits me as I open the front door. Baba is still in bed and the house is quiet. Even the lamb is still asleep in my room, his head resting on a mossy mound. I sink into my mattress and smile. Then a squeal of excitement bursts through me and I have to stifle it with my pillow. I can't believe this is happening! It's like the stars have watched my daydreams and are making my wishes come true. I close my eyes and drift to sleep, hoping they can change my destiny as well.

It seems like two minutes later I'm woken by the rattle of bones, but it's almost dark outside so I must have slept the day away. I sit up and peer through the window. The fence trembles and sways in a rush of air and a cold wave of dread rolls over me.

A great gust shakes the skulls and bones free and with a heart-wrenching clatter they fly, roll and run into the skeleton store, drawn in by a great breath from the house. The store slams shut and the house lurches suddenly upwards.

"No!" I shout, jumping out of bed and stumbling over the mossy fort. The lamb bleats loudly, bolts over his fence and goes skidding across the floor. Jack flaps up from his perch on the footboard of my bed and flies around the room, squawking. But the house is calm, already walking in long, lumbering strides.

"No! No! No!" I fling open my bedroom door. "Make it stop, Baba, please!"

Baba appears in front of me, thin wispy hair floating around her head like a halo. "What is it? What's wrong?"

"Make it stop!" I scream, tears flooding down my cheeks. The house is picking up speed, rolling along in a rhythmic canter. I drop to the floor and put my head in my hands.

Baba kneels next to me and wraps her arm around my back. "Make what stop? What is it?"

"The house!" I yell at her.

She sighs. "You know I can't do that. It must be time to move on."

"But we've only been here two weeks." This can't be happening. Not now. Benjamin was coming back,

with his big brown eyes and his easy smile. We were going to visit the town. We were going to be friends. For the first time in my life I had the courage and the opportunity to break free and explore the world beyond the fence. But now the house is taking it all away.

"I want to stay here, Baba," I sob.

"Oh, Marinka." Baba bundles me into a hug that both comforts and suffocates. The house is at full gallop now, speeding away from Benjamin and any chance of friendship I might have had, any chance of exploring that twinkling town by the lake. "You know the house has to keep moving so the living don't find The Gate. It's important—"

"But why?" I shout, pulling away from her, flushing with anger. "Why is it so important? The living all find The Gate eventually! They all die! Why does it have to be such a big secret? Why can't we stay somewhere long enough to make friends?" I glare at her, my eyes burning. She has to make the house stop, make it turn back. "The lamb!" I cry.

"You can keep the lamb," Baba says gently. "We'll have vegetable *borsch* in the spring."

"You don't understand." I can't tell her that Benjamin will be back, looking for his lamb. But all he'll find is a rocky ledge as empty as my hopes and dreams. I can't tell her how much that hurts.

"I hate this house! I hate this life!" I hear myself shouting the words, watch myself pushing Baba's hands from me. I prickle with fear because I'm not in control of my emotions or my actions. And as long as I stay in this house I will never be in control of my life, my future, or my destiny.

I run to my bedroom, throw myself onto my bed, and cry myself to sleep as the house gallops on through the night.

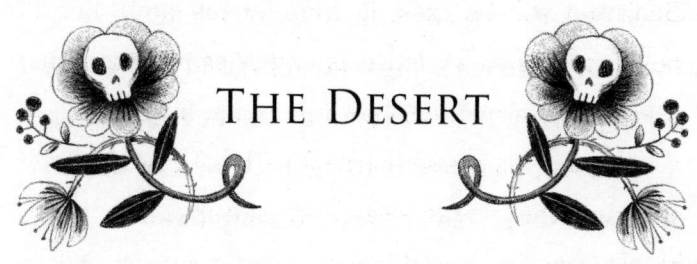

THE DESERT

Hot, dry air claws at my throat. The light from the window is dazzlingly bright. I drag myself to look at the view, shielding my eyes with a hand. Sand and more sand. A blazing sun. Heat rippling the air. Not a sign of human habitation in sight.

I exhale loudly, trying to blow sweat-damp hair from my forehead. My heart feels so heavy it might fall through my chest. Nothing has ever hurt as much as this. To have my hopes raised, then smashed to pieces, and then the pieces danced on by the stupid chicken legs of the house.

Jack taps on the window with his beak and the sash slides up. Hot air blasts in, like an oven door opening. He lifts his wings, stands for a moment scanning the horizon, and then flops gracelessly to the sand outside. Good luck finding anything to eat out there.

I sniff through a breakfast of *kasha* and damson jelly, ignoring Baba's attempts at conversation; her suggestions of having a hot sand bath, making sand art, or looking for scarab beetles and scorpions with Jack.

"Come on, Marinka, is it so bad? The dead will arrive tonight and we'll have such a party."

"It's not a party when all the guests are dead," I mumble.

"Of course it is!" A smile spreads across Baba's face and her eyes gleam with excitement. I turn away, and Baba sighs. "You said last night you want to stay somewhere long enough to make friends."

I look out of the window, my eyes stinging and my skin tight.

"Every night you have a chance to make friends," Baba says softly.

"With the dead?" I scoff.

"Yes, the dead." Baba shrugs. "Living, dead, what's the difference? People are people."

I bury my head in my hands. Living, dead, it's not

the same. It's not the same at all.

"If you would take the time to listen to them—"

"What's the point of listening to them?" My voice rises. "They're all gone by the morning!"

"If you would take the time to listen to them," Baba repeats calmly, "then you would hear their stories. Their lives would add to yours, and stay with you for ever."

"But that's not friendship!" I yell. "Friendship is having somebody really with you. To talk to and do things with. For more than one night."

"The dead have to pass through The Gate. You know that."

"So let me make friends with the living then." I stare into her eyes, challenging her, pleading with her.

"We can't do that." Baba looks away, shaking her head. "It's not the Yaga way. We have to protect the house and The Gate from the living."

"I wouldn't tell them about the house or The Gate."

"I know you wouldn't." Baba puts her hand over mine. "But it's just not safe. We have to keep the two worlds separate. That's part of our duty as Guardians."

"What if I don't want to be a Guardian?" The words that have been on my mind for so long burst free.

"Being a Guardian is your destiny."

"What if it's not?" I pull my hand away from hers. "What if I don't want it to be?"

"It is, Marinka." Baba doesn't shout but her voice gets firmer, like the strength of her words alone will convince me. "Some things just are and we can't change them." Jack wanders in and flops to the floor in the shade behind her chair. "Birds fly, fish swim, and you are the next Guardian."

"If my parents had lived—" My voice wavers and cracks.

"You would have become the next Guardian of their house. You would have had more time to prepare, but you still would have become a Guardian." Baba reaches for my hand again. "I wish they hadn't died, I really do, but I've tried to raise you as they would have. I love you just as much as they did, and I only want you to be happy."

"But I'm not," I sob. Light refracts through the tears welling in my eyes, turning the room into a kaleidoscope of stars and bubbles.

Baba squeezes my fingers. "You need to accept what you are. Being Yaga is in your blood and you can't change that. If you would focus more on the life you have instead of daydreaming about the life you don't, then I think you would be happier."

Baba's words don't help. She doesn't understand how much I need to escape all this. I stand up too fast, knocking my chair to the floor. "I'm going to feed the lamb," I snap, and storm outside to get some water from the butt.

There's no sign of life. No plants, no animals, not even a bird in the sky or an insect scurrying across the sand. No sign of water at all, and the butt is only half full. We'll be lucky if the water we have lasts a week. At least the house can't stay here for long.

The walls of the house creak and it rocks slightly, burying itself deeper into the sand, as if it heard my thoughts and wants to show me how comfortable it is here. I kick sand at it and stomp back inside to my bedroom without even stopping to warm up the water for the lamb.

Jack flaps to my shoulder and pushes his beak into my ear. I stroke him and feed him some *kozinaki*, then set about preparing a bottle for the lamb. There's not much of the special milk powder Benjamin gave me left. I hope ordinary milk powder will be all right after that.

My room is filthy and smelly, thanks to the lamb being in here all night. I guess today will be spent cleaning it out, and of course the fence will need building. Then there will be the cooking, preparing for the arrival of the dead... This can't be it, my everything, for ever. I want more. I want to explore towns and cities. I want to watch shows and concerts, go to festivals and dances. I want to meet people. I want to make friends.

I decide to call the lamb Benji, so that every time I look at him I will think of the friend I might have had if this stupid house didn't have legs. It will remind me how I feel right now; remind me that I need to find a way to escape this life.

The day goes painfully slowly. The heat is unbearable, and although I'm exhausted after I've done my chores, I can't sleep in the afternoon like I should. Even when the sun sinks low in the sky and the temperature drops, it brings me no relief.

Baba calls me to watch the sunset with her on the porch. She tells me the sky is magnificent.

"I'm stirring the *borsch*," I snap, throwing a handful of garlic into the pot.

A few minutes later Baba shuffles inside, lifts the spoon from my hand and places a tiny star-shaped pink-and-white flower on my palm. It's beautiful, and unlike anything I've ever seen before. "Did you find this out there?" I ask.

"Well, I had some help." Baba nods to Jack, who is strutting in from the porch, his chest feathers ruffling with pride. "I asked him to find a flower for my *pchelka*." Baba kisses my cheek and pulls me into a hug. My head rests on hers and it takes me by surprise how small she is. I've grown so much this year that I look down on her now.

"You shouldn't call me that. I'm not a baby any more."

"You'll always be my little bee." Baba takes the flower and tucks it behind my ear. Her familiar smell envelopes me: lavender water, bread dough, *borsch* and *kvass*. I breathe it in and some of my anger melts. It's still there, hot in my belly, but she seems to smooth the sharp edges of it away.

The dead arrive with the stars. They are very colourful this evening. Flowing robes and delicate scarves in vibrant shades. Long black hair, shiny as volcanic glass, even on the eldest dead. They add spices to the *borsch* and glitter to the air. Baba gives them guitars and they tune them in a way I've not heard before and play notes unfamiliar to my ears; mysterious runs and shimmering harmonies. The house rises and falls as the dead clap their hands and stamp their feet.

My toes become traitors, tapping the floor in time to the music as the dead dance around me. They are all smiles and laughter. I think they must have had very happy lives, and I wonder what memories bring them so much joy. I try to listen, but the language of the dead still makes no sense.

When The Gate appears, an empty feeling swells in my stomach. They are going to leave, like everyone else I meet, before I've had a chance to get to know them. Baba kisses their cheeks, speaks the death journey words and they drift away one by one. Living, dead, maybe they're the same after all. Neither hangs around for long.

I offer to clear up. I can't sleep anyway. Baba hugs me tight and goes to bed and I wander around the room, collecting bowls and glasses. I carry a basketful to wash outside.

And that's when I find her.

She's sitting on the porch steps, staring up at the sky, wearing a long green dress and scarf that are as smooth as silk and bright as spring leaves after a rain. She looks quite solid, just the very edges of her blending into the night.

Meteors streak across the sky. Baba once told me the Ancient Elders believe they are the souls of the dead on their journey. I stare at the girl, mouth open. "You aren't meant to be here. You should have gone through The Gate."

"I didn't want to."

"You have to." Even as I say the words, a question forms in my mind. *Does she? Does she really have to go?* The Gate is shut now anyway; she can't go through. This has never happened before. The dead always leave.

Then another thought strikes me, reverberating through my body like thunder.

"Say something else!" I demand, dropping the basket of dishes to the floor with a clatter.

"I don't want to leave," the girl says softly and I feel like hugging her – because even though she spoke in the language of the dead, I understood every single word.

NINA

Her name is Nina and five minutes into our conversation, I don't want her to leave either. She's smaller than me, but we're both twelve. Her hair is straight and black, mine is curly and red, but we both have a small gap between our front teeth.

We watch the shooting stars and tell each other stories we've heard about them – although I don't tell Nina the story about them being dead souls. I don't talk about death, or why Nina is here, at all.

Nina has heard that shooting stars are celestial goats dragging their hooves when they run across the sky. Most of Nina's stories involve animals. We talk for hours, joining up stars into pictures and remembering tales of constellations named after tortoises, giraffes, scorpions and snakes.

But finally, the stars fade away and the sky blushes pink. Nina rises and takes a few steps away from the porch.

"Wait! Where are you going?" I reach for her arm, but of course my hand passes right through it.

She stops anyway and stares out at the endless sand, eyebrows crinkled. "I'm not sure," she whispers. "I don't know where I am."

"There's nothing out there." I wave my hand at the desert. "Stay here, with me." My mind is thrumming with ideas; how she can hide in my room at night when The Gate is open, then we can spend time together in the day, talking, playing games, and when the house moves on we can explore new landscapes together...

"I'm supposed to... I need to..."

"Come and see my lamb," I say quickly.

"You have a lamb?"

"He's an orphan. I'm hand-rearing him." I pick up the basket of dishes I dropped earlier and beckon Nina round to Benji's shelter on the back porch. I moved him there while I was cleaning my room yesterday and he fell asleep snuggled into one of my old shawls. He wakes up when he hears us and squeezes his head through the gap near the water butt, eager for a stroke and some milk.

"He's so cute!" Nina smiles as she tickles Benji under the chin and he tries to lick her fingers. "We used to have a camel, but my father sold him a few years ago. We moved to a new white house on the edge of the desert." Nina's smile widens as memories of her life flood back. "There was a well, and my father dug little channels to send the water over the ground. He planted figs, jojoba, tiny orange trees and magaria. He even planted oleanders because my mother loved the flowers so much." Her face darkens with sorrow. "My mother. She got ill first. Then my sisters. Then me..." Her eyes narrow as she tries to remember. "Why am I here?"

I drape my shawl around her, like I've seen Baba do to the dead who don't want to pass through The Gate. It's strange how my shawl can comfort her but I can't touch her with my hands. Baba says it's something to do with the house. It gives the dead energy for their journey, so they can seem almost real. They end up being lifelike in some ways, but not in others, and it varies between souls, and even from moment to moment. Like how, during the guidings, the dead can eat and drink, even though their bodies aren't really here, but then they float weightlessly to the stars.

I finish washing the dishes and stack them in the basket to dry. "Would you like some *kasha*?" I ask. "Porridge," I correct, when Nina looks at me in confusion.

Footsteps echo through the house. Baba is awake, humming a happy tune.

"Shhhh." My finger rushes to my lips as the rest of my body freezes. "Stay here with Benji. I'll bring some out for you," I whisper.

The door creaks so loudly I wonder if the house knows about Nina and is trying to give me away. I push it open quickly, my hands hot with annoyance. Every time I have a chance at friendship the house tries to ruin it.

"You're up early." Baba kisses my cheeks.

"I was checking on the lamb." I look away, hoping

she doesn't notice the blood rushing into my face. "Can I eat my breakfast with him outside? It's such a lovely morning."

"Of course." Baba smiles. "It's nice to see you've cheered up a bit since yesterday."

I nod guiltily and set about making a bottle for Benji, and *kasha* for me and Nina. I stir up a huge panful of the porridge, grate chocolate over the top, and sneak an extra spoon into my pocket.

Nina and I eat with Benji on the back porch. I'm so glad I built this shelter for him in one of the house's deaf spots. If the house does know about Nina, at least it can't hear us talking. Jack joins us, and as he sucks *kasha* from my fingers, like he used to do when he was a chick, I tell Nina how I found and raised him.

"Do you have any brothers or sisters?" she asks.

"No." I shake my head. "I just live here with my grandmother. My parents died when I was a baby."

"I have five sisters." Nina groans. "There's never any peace and quiet."

"I'd like that. It's far too quiet around here." I bite my lip as I hear Baba still humming inside the house.

Nina stares into the distance and she seems to fade slightly. "I don't know how to get home, to my sisters."

"Our house moves," I jump in brightly. "Perhaps it can take you home."

"Really?" Nina's eyebrows crinkle.

"Maybe." I turn to Jack, flushing with the lie. "I don't think we'll stay here long, a week or two at most. Then the house will take us somewhere new. The jungle, or the mountains, or the seaside."

"You've seen the ocean?" Her eyes light up.

"Of course."

"What's it like?" She leans forward eagerly.

"It's like the desert in some ways. Endless water instead of endless sand. The waves move like dunes, only faster. Salty spray stings your face, like sand in the wind."

"But it must be so different too."

"Yes, it's cool and fresh and—"

"Wet?" Nina suggests.

"Yes, it's very wet." I laugh.

"Can you make your house go there next? I'd love to see the ocean."

I wish I could. Maybe Nina would forget about wanting to go home if I showed her the ocean. "The house decides where it goes," I admit reluctantly. "But it often goes to the coast," I rush in as her face falls. "Not long ago it settled on a tiny island. The ocean was all around, as far as you could see. It changed colour a hundred times a day, depending on the sky and the light. Waves washed onto the shore, knocking pebbles up and down the beach. The dead—" I stop myself.

"The dead?" she asks.

I was going to say how the dead walked right across the surface of the ocean, but I think of another memory to cover my tracks. "Lots of dead jellyfish washed up one day, all transparent and squidgy. Jack ate one and got sick."

Jack ruffles his feathers and turns away.

"Silly bird." Nina laughs. "He's lovely. You're so lucky to have a pet."

"He's not really a pet. He can take care of himself now. When he learned to fly I thought he would go away, but he always comes back. I'm glad he does."

"Do you think he will stay with you for ever now?" she asks.

"I hope so." I look at Jack and a lump forms in my throat. Nothing is for ever. Everything moves on; the living, the dead, the house. I push the thought to the back of my mind and stand up. "Would you like to check the fence with me?"

Nina nods and I lead her to the far corner, out of sight of the house and its windows. I scan the perimeter to check none of the bones have fallen. I tell Nina the fence is a tradition, like I told Benjamin. She looks at the skulls and shivers. "None of our customs are as strange as this."

For a moment I see the fence and the house through Nina's eyes. Empty skulls balanced on bleached bones. Warped wooden walls leading to a twisted roof with a crooked chimney. The balustrade round the porch bends up and down at odd angles,

and dry sand has been kicked into untidy piles where the house's legs have buried themselves.

I think about Nina's description of her house. Clean and white and surrounded by the colours and scents of beautiful flowers. I see how my house must seem strange to her, frightening even. I turn my back on the house and clamber over the fence.

"Come on." I beckon to Nina. "Let's go for a walk."

As my feet hit the ground on the other side of the fence, a rush of excitement runs through me. Right now I don't care about disobeying Baba. I don't even care about the fact I might get caught. All I can think about is the joy of escaping, even if it will only be for a little while.

I kick off my shoes and let the sand flow between my toes as we walk away from the house. A huge golden sun sits low on the horizon, warming the still air. Nina stops and crouches next to a small circular pit, no bigger than my palm. "It's an ant lion trap."

She points at the centre. "Buried in there is an ant lion; an insect with huge spiky jaws. It waits, hiding at the bottom, for an ant to come along."

"And the ant just falls into the pit?" I wonder why the ant wouldn't walk around it.

"It slips down the steep sides, and the ant lion throws sand at it. The ant struggles to escape but it can't." Nina's voice lowers dramatically and her fingers mime the struggles of the ant. "It slides further, pulled down by the sand, and eventually it reaches the ant lion's jaws." Nina's hands slap shut and she laughs.

"Do you want to watch it for a while? See if an ant comes along?"

We sit on the sand, staring at the trap. "If an ant comes, shall we save it? You know, at the last minute?" I ask.

"That's what my sister used to do." Nina smiles. "You can if you want, but then the ant lion won't get its meal. You know, the ant lion is really a larva. If it eats enough, it changes into a beautiful dragonfly-like creature, with four speckled wings and eyes that glow silver when it flies at dusk."

"Hmmm." I'm not sure what to do now. I don't want to stop the ant lion becoming a beautiful dragonfly, but I don't want to watch an ant die either. I'm relieved when no ants come along.

The sun climbs higher in the sky and waves of heat shimmer on the horizon. It's too hot for ants now; they would fry on this sand before they even got to the ant lion trap. My heart sinks as I realize I'm going to have to go back to the house for some shade.

I sneak Nina into my bedroom while the house sleeps and Baba naps in front of the empty fireplace, her *balalaika* cradled in her arms. A cool draught flows into the room as the chimney breast rises and falls, gently breathing in air. The house might be old and strange, but at least it takes care of Baba. I shut my door softly, so I don't wake either of them.

The window is open, heat flooding in. Jack sits on the sill, looking out across the desert, eyes half closed and wings slightly raised in the hope of catching a breeze. Nina and I sit on the floor below him and I show her how to play chequers, and she teaches me a game where we have to guess what the other is thinking.

I'm not very good at it and I doze off in the heat while trying to think of an orange flower she has in her mind.

When I wake, the air is soft and cool. Nina is staring out of the window. The skull candles are already lit, throwing yellow light and dark shadows across the empty sand. I hear Baba, singing and preparing food for the dead.

A weight falls across my chest and I struggle to breathe. Nina shouldn't have to go through The Gate if she doesn't want to, and I shouldn't have to lose another friend. The house is trying to control both of our lives. It's not fair.

I draw my curtains to block Nina's view of the beckoning skulls, give her a book to read, and make her promise not leave my room under any circumstances.

But as I go to help Baba prepare for the guiding, I can't shake an image from my mind; of The Gate opening and pulling Nina inside, like an ant being pulled into an ant lion trap. The thought of losing her makes my blood run cold, and I don't know how to stop it from happening. Just like I don't know how to control my own destiny.

Learning
to Swim

Baba has made *ukha* from tinned catfish and vegetables. Wood crackles in the hearth and flames lick up the sides of the cauldron. The heat and the smell of fish and spices mingle with my thoughts of losing Nina, making me feel queasy.

"Tonight we'll treat the desert dead to a fish supper." Baba nods at the table and smiles. It's already laid with *kvass* and glasses, and bowls of food with a decidedly fishy theme: pickled herring with soured cream from the cold pantry, blinis with smoked salmon and dill, salted dried *vobla*, and mini fish dumplings. There is nothing left for me to do, so I sit and help myself to a blini, hoping it will unknot my stomach.

"Did you sleep well?" Baba asks.

I nod. "I'm sorry I didn't help with the cooking."

"It's fine." Baba looks at me intently and I wonder if she suspects anything. I shift in my seat and gaze across the table.

"The food looks lovely."

"Makes a change from *borsch*." Baba sips the fish broth and adds more pepper. "Tell me the death journey words."

"I don't know them." I frown, thinking about how I don't *want* to know them. I've heard the death journey words a thousand times, and every time I've done my best to ignore them.

"Try," Baba urges. "The nightingale that sings finds a song."

I groan and stumble over the words. "*May you have strength on the long and arduous journey ahead. The stars are waiting for you.*"

"*Calling for you*," Baba corrects.

"*Move on with gratitude for your time on Earth.*" I rub my temples to make it seem like I'm trying to remember.

"Every moment now an eternity," Baba whispers.

"With infinite value?' I ask, my thoughts drifting to Nina. How lovely it would be to show her the ocean...

"You carry with you memories of infinite value." Baba nods. "And then..."

"The bit that always changes is next." I stuff the last piece of blini into my mouth, in the hope it will stop Baba asking me anything else.

"That's right." Baba smiles. "Then you explain what the soul has gained from their life and is taking to the stars. It is often the love of family or friends, but there is an endless variety of gifts the dead take with them: the power of music, the excitement of discovery, the light of hope..."

Baba goes on but my mind wanders again. If I spend my life guiding the dead, how will I ever gain anything to take to the stars myself?

"Marinka?" Baba swings back into focus as she adds a plate of spiced honey bread to the table.

"Pardon?" I murmur.

"Do you remember the last words?"

I shake my head and sigh.

"Peace at returning to the stars." Baba makes a sweeping circle with her hands. *"The great cycle is complete."*

An uncomfortable heat prickles the back of my neck as Baba entwines her fingers tightly together and looks right into my eyes. "The cycle needs to complete."

My heart beats faster and I feel like I might be sick. She knows. She knows about Nina. I look away, wiping my sweaty palms on my skirt.

"That's why Guardians are so important. We have a responsibility to help souls complete their journey. To return to the stars from whence they came."

"What if they don't?" I ask quietly, my whole head tingling.

Baba's jaw drops open in shock. Maybe she doesn't know about Nina after all. "Why, they would be lost for ever!" She gasps, as if that would be the absolute worst thing in the whole universe.

I lift a piece of honey bread from the plate and pick crumbs off it. I'm not hungry, just trying to distract myself. I don't want to think about what Baba just said.

"I think you should say the death journey words this evening." Baba nods slowly. "I think you should guide someone through The Gate."

"No, I can't." I shake both my head and my hands quickly. "I'm not ready."

"Sometimes the best way to learn is to jump in." Baba smiles, her whiskers and teeth pointing out at all angles. "Remember when you learned to swim?"

I roll my eyes and groan. The house had been settled on a sheer cliff overlooking a deep lagoon, with warm azure water and white sunlight dappling the surface. Baba kept asking me to try to swim, but I didn't want to get my face wet.

One day I was standing on the cliff, looking out over the lagoon to the ocean beyond, when the house lifted itself up, stretched out one of its long spindly legs, and kicked me into the water. I screamed in free fall and landed hard in the strange echoing silence of the underwater world. After what seemed like an eternity of struggling, I burst up through the surface, gasping for air and desperately reaching for something solid. There was nothing to hold on to; no floor beneath me, nothing but sky above.

My face kept sinking beneath the waves. The more I thrashed, the more I was pulled down. After swallowing several mouthfuls of salty water, I took one last breath of air and let myself drop beneath the surface.

I opened my eyes, blinked, and all my panic ebbed away. It was so calm and peaceful, so blue and endless. Flecks of silt hung suspended in the water, illuminated by columns of sunlight. I began to move, slowly and smoothly, as I had watched the turtles do in the mornings. My limbs propelled me gently forwards, so I used the same pattern but kicked harder. Soon I was flying through the water, moving up to gulp air, then descending back beneath the surface and gliding towards the shore.

Every day after that I swam, face under the water, eyes open. But I didn't forgive the house for a long time. If I'm honest, I'm not sure I ever did. I was so cross that I ignored the vine swings the house grew for me and its claws when they poked me to play tag.

I don't remember playing with the house at all after that day. All of a sudden I miss the times when I was younger, and the house and I were friends. But then I remember what the house did and anger bubbles up inside me again.

"That could have killed me," I say to both Baba, and the house.

"Nonsense!" Baba laughs, then shakes her head. "The house was watching over you, and you know how well it can swim. You were never in any danger." She pats the chimney breast tenderly. "The house will always take care of you, Marinka. You should know that by now."

The door creaks open and the first of the dead drifts in. It's a translucent old man, wide-eyed and pale. Baba rushes to him, beaming. Words pour from her mouth and though I try to focus, my mind is spinning with thoughts of Nina, the great cycle, returning to the stars, and the panic I felt when I sank beneath the blue lagoon before I was ready to swim.

More of the dead arrive; wispy and solid, quiet and talkative. I'm curious to find out if I will understand any of them, the way I understand Nina. But I don't. Not properly. I get a hazy impression of their thoughts and memories conveyed by body language and facial expressions. Maybe the odd word here and there. It's not like with Nina at all.

Nina. I feel like I should check on her, but I don't want to open my bedroom door in case she is pulled away. The Gate is open now, the dead disappearing one by one.

"Marinka," Baba calls. She's holding a cobweb of a man, guiding him slowly to The Gate. I know what she wants. She wants me to say the death journey words and send him on his way. She's picked this old man because he's so ready his soul is practically on the journey already. He has a faraway look in his eyes, like he sees the stars and his place with them.

I turn my back on Baba, pretend I didn't hear her, and wander around the room, serving spirit *trost* and false smiles. I don't want to guide anyone through The Gate. Not the old man, and certainly not Nina.

Straightening my spine, I take a deep breath and tell myself I can't be forced into guiding the way the house forced me to learn how to swim. And although I feel a sharp pang of guilt for ignoring Baba, the rush of power at taking control of my life, if only for a short time, makes it all worthwhile.

SERINA

When I return to my room hours later, Nina looks fainter, more nebulous, her edges floating into the air like steam. Baba's words from earlier run through my mind – *they would be lost for ever* – but I push them away and lead Nina outside to play while Baba and the house sleep.

We spin cartwheels in the sand and squander water building sandcastles. Maybe the dwindling supplies in the butt will encourage the house to move on to somewhere where it rains. Like the coast.

If the house were to move near the ocean, maybe Nina would be so happy she would forget about her past. When she talks about her family she gets sad and wants to go home. She doesn't realize she can't.

She doesn't realize she's dead.

There's an unsettling ache in my stomach. As much as I'm trying to distract Nina from her memories, I'm trying to distract myself from the thought that at some point I should probably tell her truth. But then I'll lose her. Is it so bad to want to have a friend for more than one night?

I keep leading our conversations back to the present, or the future. We talk about the things we want to do when we grow up. She wants to be a farmer, like her father, growing food and flowers in the desert, filling dry and empty sand with life. She says if you plant the right seeds you can cultivate not only plants, but soil, water, insects, birds and animals. She says you can create whole worlds by planting tiny seeds and nurturing what grows.

She asks me what I want to be. I don't tell her I'm destined to be the next Guardian. I imagine that my future is undecided; that I could be an artist like Benjamin, or a teacher, or an actress in a theatre. I think of all the jobs I've read about in books that involve working with the living, enjoying life, and my heart swells. Then I imagine that I could live in a normal house, a house without legs, and stay in one place and make friends.

When the sun rises high overhead the house begins to stir. Its front door yawns lazily and its legs stretch out over the hot sand. We retreat to the shade and privacy of the back porch and feed Benji, while throwing scraps of food up into the air for Jack to catch until he tires of us and hides on the roof in the shadow of the chimney.

I tell Baba I'm reading *The Book of Yaga* – the crumbly old guidebook for Yaga, so she starts cooking without me, and Nina shows me bustards flying on the horizon in the late afternoon. Her eyes light up as she remembers chameleons and cobras she found in her garden, and how her father once showed her the burrow of a desert fox, and I have to distract her again before she gets homesick. I talk about the crashing waves of the ocean, and giant whales that breach the surface after a storm.

Dusk comes all too soon and I sneak Nina back into my room through the window and leave to light the skulls. I feel heavy. I tell myself it's tiredness, but I know in my heart it's something far deeper. Something to do with Nina, and not telling her the truth.

The first of the dead to arrive looks so much like Nina I panic, thinking she's left my room to find The Gate. But the girl is a few years older. She has the same long dark hair and shining copper eyes. The same look of confusion, like she's lost and her memories are just out of reach. Baba wraps a shawl around her, ushers her to the table and pours her a drink of *kvass*.

"You are dead, my child," Baba says brightly. I turn to her in surprise because I understood her perfectly, even though she's speaking in the language of the dead. "You're here to celebrate your life and move on with joy. You're about to leave this Earth and embark on a long journey to return to your place in the stars."

The girl stares at Baba and catches her infectious smile. "I'm dead?" she repeats uncertainly.

"Yes. Your time on Earth is over and you're here to prepare for the death journey. It will be both challenging and wonderful, but before you go we can celebrate your life and memories. Would you like some *borsch*? Marinka, could you get some *borsch* for our guest, please? What is your name, child?"

"Serina. I was ill." Her eyes narrow as she tries to remember. "Like my mother, and my sisters."

I drop the ladle into the cauldron. She sounds just like Nina.

"How many sisters did you have?" Baba asks.

"Five. Thank you." Serina takes the bowl from me and sniffs the steaming red liquid. "We lived on the edge of the desert. My father planted oleanders all around the house."

It is Nina's sister. It has to be. I glance over to my bedroom door. The handle turns slowly and a crack widens between the door and the frame. I rush over and squeeze myself inside, pushing Nina back. She looks at me, wide-eyed and curious.

"I thought I heard my sister."

"No." I shake my head vigorously. "They're my grandmother's friends. You have to stay in here."

"But it sounds like her." She leans around me, like an invisible string is pulling her to the door.

"It's not," I snap, then take a deep breath and try

to speak calmly. "Please stay in here, Nina. Watch Jack for me," I add as I notice him pacing along the footboard of the bed. "I'll bring you some scraps to feed him in a little while."

Nina nods reluctantly, her gaze still drawn to the door.

"Promise?" I press. "It's important."

Nina looks at me and sighs. "I promise."

I shut the door and rush straight over to Baba, practically dragging her away from the dead woman she's now talking to. "I want to guide Serina through The Gate," I whisper urgently.

Baba looks at me in surprise. "That's wonderful, but The Gate isn't even open yet."

I look past the gathering dead to the corner of the room where The Gate always appears and stifle a groan.

"If you really want to help, the first stage is to listen." Baba nods over to where Serina sits, daintily nibbling some *chak-chak*. "Let her tell you her memories and relive her time on Earth. She'll only be ready to move on once she's identified what she's gained from this life and said her goodbyes."

My eyebrows fall. Why does guiding have to be so complicated? Why can't I just say the death journey words and send her on her way?

"Go on." Baba nudges me towards Serina. "It's easy. Ask her about her life. And listen to her. Really listen."

I walk slowly over to Serina. "Hello." I smile uncomfortably. "I'm Marinka."

"I'm Serina." She smiles back, looking so much like Nina I feel like I know her already.

"So…" I try to think of what to ask, hoping this won't take long. I want Serina to go through The Gate as quickly as possible, so Nina doesn't hear her, and come looking for her. "You lived near the desert?"

"Yes." Serina starts talking and the strangest thing happens. She tells me about her house and her family – all things I've heard from Nina – but as she does so, my house and the dead crowded around the table and the fire all fade away, until I can barely see them. It's like part of me is literally transported into Serina's garden. I feel earth beneath my feet, smell flowers as if they are right under my nose, and hear the rustle and chirp of birds hiding in the leaves.

Then I feel her emotions. My heart races as she chases swallowtails, and bursts with joy when her sisters are born. I have to clench my teeth to stop from crying out when I feel her mother die. I wonder if this is what Baba meant when she said the dead's lives would add to mine. If it is, I don't like it. It's frightening, having someone else's memories and feelings inside my head.

"It's time." Baba touches my arm and the house swings back into focus. The Gate is open, everything in the room bending towards it. Far away, almost imperceptible in the darkness, galaxies swirl and nebulae erupt with colour.

"What do you take with you to the stars?" Baba asks Serina.

"The love of my family and home," she replies without question, and it makes such perfect sense that I clap my hands together. That's what I feel too, that's what the lasting impression of her life is.

Baba kisses Serina on both cheeks and nods to me.

I know what I have to do. I lead Serina to The Gate, the death journey words flowing from my mouth without hesitation. *"May you have strength on the long and arduous journey ahead. The stars are calling for you. Move on with gratitude for your time on Earth. Every moment now an eternity. You carry with you memories of infinite value, the love of your family and home."* Serina steps into The Gate and drifts away into the darkness. *"Peace at returning to the stars. The great cycle is complete."*

Clouds roll above me and an ocean washes far below. Rainbows flash across the glassy mountains. I feel like I recognize this place, like I've been here before. It's a memory so tangible, yet just out of reach. I lean into The Gate, thinking it will help me remember, but Baba yanks me back with so much force my shoulder joint pops.

"You must never cross the threshold!" Baba's wrinkles fall into a deep frown. "You must never step into The Gate."

An icy shiver runs along my bones. I've never seen Baba look so stern, and I prickle with the sensation that I've brushed against some great disaster and only just survived. But I don't understand the danger, or Baba's reaction, or the strange feeling I had when I leaned into The Gate.

JUST A FEW MORE MINUTES

I sit on the porch steps, watching meteors fall through a deep blue sky, wondering if one of them is Serina on her journey. The front door creaks open and Baba shuffles out. She passes me two mugs of hot cocoa, grasps the balustrade and it bends, helping to lower her down, as the steps rise up to meet her.

"Do you want me to get you a cushion?" I offer.

"No, I'm fine." Her bones creak as she settles onto the step beside me. "You did well tonight. I'm proud of you." She takes one of the mugs from my hands, smiles, and brushes my cheek. I frown and pull away. I only wanted to guide Serina into The Gate so Nina didn't find her. That's nothing to be proud of.

Baba sips her cocoa and looks out across the desert.

A band of orange light is thickening on the horizon, throwing dark shadows from the ripples in the sand. I'm glad Baba doesn't say anything else. So many thoughts and emotions are swirling through my mind, I feel like a single word might be enough to spin me out of control.

I didn't want to guide. I didn't even think I could. Now that I have, I wonder if it means being a Guardian is a destiny I will never escape.

All my daydreams of friends and futures unknown crumble away as I imagine life as a Guardian stretching ahead of me once more, long and straight. Always stuck in this house. Every night being weighed down by the memories of the dead before I lead them away. A life of goodbyes. And when Baba moves on, being alone as a Guardian. The thought makes me feel as cold and desolate as the desert at night.

"Guiding is tiring." Baba reaches out and strokes my hair before lifting the empty mug from my hands. "You should get some sleep."

"I will, Baba. Just a few more minutes with the sunrise." I feel her looking at me but I can't meet her gaze. I wonder if she senses all the unsaid words swarming in the silence between us. She might feel proud of me, but I'm ashamed of myself. She might think I'm a step closer to becoming the next Guardian, but it's something I never want to be. I need a different future. One I can shape and mould myself. But I don't know how to make her understand that.

Baba kisses my cheek, wishes me sweet dreams and moves to lift herself from the porch. The balustrade bends down to her and Baba pats it affectionately. "Thank you, House," she murmurs. The balustrade straightens, helping Baba up, and she shuffles back indoors.

As soon as the door swings shut there's a tapping on my bedroom window. The sash slides open and Jack flaps clumsily to my feet. He croaks a greeting and nuzzles his neck against my ankles. His show of affection blurs my eyes. I don't feel worthy of his love right now.

"Go on." I gently push him away. "See if you can find a scorpion or something." He tilts his head and stares at me with his bright silver eyes. "Go on!" I push him a little harder and he squawks angrily and struts off, ruffling his feathers at the injustice of my snub.

I groan, frustrated with myself for so many reasons: for lying to Nina, for selfishly guiding Serina, for not being able to explain to Baba how I feel, and now for being mean to Jack.

The house creaks and the steps twist beneath me. "What?" I snap, my frustration turning into anger. "What do you want now?" I put my hands on the floor in an effort to balance as the house swivels me round on its steps so I have a perfect view of my bedroom window.

Nina is sitting on the sill, fading into the dawn light. Her edges are vague and I can almost see right through her. The silhouette of my oil lamp is visible inside her chest. She looks empty, lost and confused. Guilt squeezes my belly.

"All right." I scowl at the porch steps. "I'll tell her." But as soon as I say the words I want to take them back. My heartbeat quickens and my palms sweat. I don't want Nina to know I kept the truth from her, and I don't want her to go.

"I'll tell her," I repeat craftily, a plan forming in my mind, "if you take us to the seaside first."

The house sinks into the sand and the windows blink shut.

"Please?" I rise and rest my forehead against the gnarled wood near the front door. The wall feels cold and contracts away from my touch. I stamp a foot on the porch. "Please," I say firmly. "I've never asked you for anything. Let me show her the ocean, then I promise I'll tell her. I'll even guide her through The Gate myself. Just let me show her the ocean first."

The house sighs and tilts forward to stretch its legs.

"Thank you." I beam, a wave of relief and happiness washing over me. "Jack!" I look around and spot him digging near the fence. He turns his back on me and continues to flick through the sand with his beak and claws. "Come on, Jack, we're leaving."

He ignores me.

I roll my eyes. "All right. I'm sorry," I say with a flourish of my arm. He slowly turns and ambles back to the house without making eye contact, ruffling his feathers dramatically as he passes me by.

The skeleton store opens and the fence bones rush into it with a clatter. Then the house surges upwards, and begins to walk. I hold my arms out to balance as I sway into my bedroom. "We're going to the coast." I almost sing the words, too loudly in my excitement.

Nina stares at me in confusion. It seems to take a few moments for her to remember who I am, and for my words to make sense, but then she smiles and fills with colour. "Really?" she asks.

"Really." I nod, my face aching from a huge smile. "I'm going to show you the ocean."

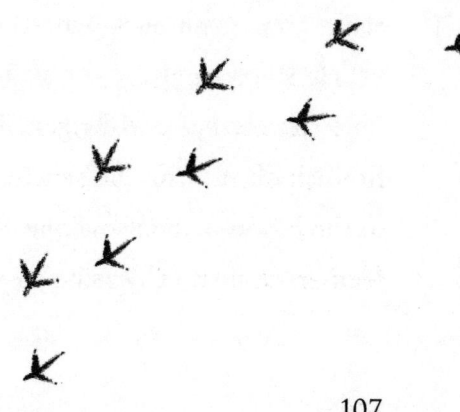

THE BEACH

I've never seen the house travel in the daytime before, and never shared a journey with a friend. Laughter shakes my body and a feeling of weightlessness dizzies my mind. My promise to the house is forgotten, left behind in the desert.

Nina and I sit at the window, watching landscapes fly past. The house gallops over the desert, kicking up a cloud of fine sand behind it. It heaves itself over steep grey mountains, bounds down into a lush green valley, steps carefully through a jungle, and emerges onto the gleaming white sand of a long narrow beach in the early afternoon.

The house settles at one end of the beach, the front door just a few paces from the sea. It stretches its long legs out, carefully lowers its huge chicken feet into the water and sighs with pleasure.

A cool breeze flows in through the windows, carrying the sharp, fresh smells of salt water and sea creatures. Nina's eyes are huge, reflecting the scene with added sparkle.

"Can we go to the water?" she asks eagerly.

"Soon." I nod. "Let me check on my grandmother first."

Baba is still asleep, but I know she'll wake soon so I make sugared black tea, and slice bread and *kolbasa*. I take some to Nina, with a little extra for Jack as a peace offering, and go to feed Benji a bottle. When I return, Baba is sipping her tea on the porch and gazing at the ocean. Her white hair drifts out from under her headscarf like a cloud.

"Isn't it beautiful? I didn't expect to wake here." She pats the balustrade fondly. "Maybe the house got hot feet in the desert and needed to cool off."

I nod, wondering how I can get Baba back into the house so Nina and I can sneak off. "What are you cooking today?" I ask.

"I thought we could have the day off." Baba links her arm through mine. "We could go for a swim, laze on the beach, and cook on a campfire under the stars tonight, just me and you."

"But the dead!" My voice rises. "The guiding!"

"Everyone needs a day off now and then. If we don't light the skulls, the dead will go to other Yaga houses. For one night, it will be fine." Baba hops from one leg to the other in an excited little dance. "I haven't seen the house soak its feet in years. I think it's a sign. Come on, let's go skinny-dipping!"

"No! We have to guide. I..." I clutch the first excuse that comes to mind. "I only just guided my first dead soul. I want to make sure I can do it again."

"Of course you'll be able to. But look at this place." Baba lifts her arms, like she's presenting me with the beach as a gift. "I think the house has brought you here to celebrate your first guiding. Let's have a day of rest and fun." She raises her eyebrows and smiles.

I look at the floor. "I just want today to be normal. I want you to cook for the dead while I build the fence. That's what we always do. I don't want to go skinny-dipping or laze on the beach." The words leave a sour taste in my mouth, because they are big fat lies. I do want to swim and sunbathe, but I want to do it with Nina, not Baba.

"What's wrong?" Baba asks softly.

"Nothing," I snap. "You're the one always telling me I should guide the dead, but now I actually want to, you think something is wrong."

Baba's face falls. Her legs stop bouncing and she stoops back over like an old woman. My heart feels like it's being pulled out. Maybe this is what it feels like to be heartless: all cold and empty inside. I push the feeling away and stomp off the porch.

Ignoring the beautiful blue sky, the soft white sands and the calmly lapping waves, I march over to the skeleton store and drag out the bones for the fence.

"Marinka?" Baba calls after me but I ignore her. I push a femur into the sand, my hands shaking. "I didn't mean to upset you," she says. "We can guide if you want."

I nod, but I'm too ashamed to look at her. I carry on building the fence.

"I'll cook then." She shuffles across the porch and the door swings shut.

A tear rolls down my cheek and I brush it away, scratching my skin with sand. I'll make it up to Baba. I promise myself I will. I can spend time with her another day. Not today though. Today has to be about me and Nina. I have to show her the ocean. It is my last chance to spend time with her before she disappears through The Gate for ever.

I carry some bones past my bedroom window, and whisper to Nina that we'll be able to go and explore as soon as I've built the fence. She smiles wide, her eyes glittering with sunshine and excitement, and this unknots some of the guilt inside me. Working with the bones calms me too, and I convince myself I'm doing the right thing. It's like I'm making Nina's final wish come true. Even Baba would understand that, I think.

Baba steps out and asks me if I want some food, but I tell her I'm not hungry. Then she says she's going to have a nap before dusk. She retreats indoors and plays a slow and sorrowful tune on her flute for a while before silence descends over the house. I wait another half-hour, to be sure she's asleep, then sneak Nina outside.

We walk along the shore until we're hidden from the windows by huge drooping palm trees. Nina kicks off her sandals and walks into the gentle frothing waves rolling onto the sand.

She giggles and wiggles her toes. "Oh, this is wonderful!"

I smile back at her. Seeing Nina this happy is brilliant. If only Baba hadn't been so disappointed that I didn't want to spend the day with her, then I might be able to shake the ache from my chest.

"Look!" Nina squeals as another wave rolls in, bringing tiny fish that dart between her toes. I take off my shoes and jump over the waves with her, pushing Baba to the back of my mind. Then we wander along the shore, looking at shells glistening in the sand, and sea creatures tucked up in calm areas of the shallows.

Nina has never seen sea urchins or starfish. Each time I show her something new, her eyes light up with wonder and I feel her delight burst through me, as if I were seeing them for the first time too. We wade deeper, until we're up to our necks in the warm, silky water.

"This is amazing!" Nina beams, her face shiny, her long hair and green scarf swirling around her like kelp.

"Try lifting your feet off the bottom." I kick my legs up and show Nina how to float on her back like driftwood bobbing on the surface. She copies me and we lie side by side, looking up at the bright blue sky with the seabirds dipping in and out of view. The waves roll beneath us, lifting us gently up and down, and water flows around my ears. I hear the echoes of the ocean beneath us and Nina's sighs of pleasure.

"I never imagined so much water." Nina rolls onto her belly and her face dips under the waves. "It's so salty."

"It's all right though, you get used to it. Come with me, and keep your eyes open." I sink beneath the surface facing Nina and she joins me, blinking repeatedly until she focuses on my face and smiles. I point down and swim deeper, further out from the shore. I show Nina feathery plants growing on the rippled seabed, crabs scuttling across the sand, and fish swimming peacefully around glowing pillars of light. An octopus appears from nowhere and darts away from us in a cloud of dark ink.

"Was that an octopus?" Nina asks when we burst back through the surface. "I've only ever heard stories about them. I wasn't even sure they were real. Can we follow it?"

We plunge back under the waves and try to follow the octopus, but it's too fast for us. We end up chasing each other through the water instead, in an explosion of bubbles and light. I laugh so much my sides ache, and swallow so much salt water that my nose and throat sting.

Soon I'm shivering. The water is cooler, and the waves are lifting us higher and pulling us lower than before. The thin line of the beach seems to be retreating into the distance. I show Nina how to ride the waves back to shore, and we sit on the sand behind some rocks, letting the last of the sun's rays warm and dry us.

As the sun sinks into the jungle behind the beach, the shadow of the house stretches over us, cold and dark. Goosebumps shiver across my skin. I don't want to go back. I know the house will hold me to my promise; it will show Nina to Baba, and force her into

The Gate. I pull my shawl tight around me and tug on Nina's scarf.

"Let's walk this way," I say, and pull her further along the beach, away from the house, and The Gate.

The coast seems to extend for ever, stretching on into the night. A cold wet wind blows off the sea and waves crash alongside us, churning up sand and smashing the water into foam. A few times I think I see creatures writhing in the surf like dark, tangled eels, but Nina says I'm imagining it.

An orange glow appears on the horizon, and as we draw closer I make out individual lights, distorted and reflected in the ocean.

"It must be a town, or a city." I try to judge the size of the settlement, wondering how many living people are there, and if it has a market, a library, or a theatre...

"I'm cold," Nina whispers.

I take off my shawl and drape it over her shoulders. It falls straight through her, pooling on the sand at her feet. I stare at Nina in surprise. She's barely there. I suppose I've been aware of her fading, but it still comes as a shock to see her so, well, dead.

Nina looks at the shawl on the floor and wraps her arms around her chest. "What's happening to me?" Her eyes are wide and transparent. I see the stars in the night sky behind them.

"Nothing," I answer quickly, raising my hand to reach for hers. I lower it again as I remember I can't touch her.

A gust of wind makes me shudder. Something in the jungle screams. What am I doing? Even if we get to the town, what then? It's the middle of the night. I should be at home, with Baba, Jack and Benji. I've left them all behind, and for what? Nina is dead. And she's fading away even faster than before. She belongs through The Gate. I look at her and think back to what Benjamin said about being lonely even when you're with people, and I realize that, even though I'm with Nina, I feel completely alone.

I glance back in the direction of the house. It's been hours since dusk but Baba can't have lit the skulls. I would see their glow in the distance if she had. I think I smell *ukha* on the breeze, but it's probably just the smell of the ocean. All of a sudden, more than anything, I want to go home. I want to have Baba pull me into a hug, and feel the house sway beneath my feet.

"Should we be going that way?" Nina follows my gaze along the shore towards the house hidden somewhere in the darkness. "I feel like we should be going that way." She looks at her hands. Her fingers have almost disappeared completely. "What's happening to me?" she asks again, her voice shaky.

There's no easy way to say the words. My throat tightens. "You're dead," I whisper. As soon as the words slip out of my mouth, it's like a weight has been lifted from my shoulders.

"Oh." She nods. She doesn't seem as surprised as I thought she would be.

I stare at my feet and dig my toes into the sand. "I'm sorry, I should have told you before." Once I start talking, I can't stop. I tell her about the house, The Gate, and the guiding of the dead. I tell her she was meant to celebrate her life and prepare for her journey but I didn't help her because I wanted her to stay and be my friend. I tell her how lonely it can be living in a house with chicken legs when you only ever meet the dead, and they have to move on every night. I apologize over and over, but it doesn't make me feel any better. In fact it makes my insides tighten even more, hearing the truth out loud. I go on until I've no words left to say and I'm just staring at her, lost in the moonlight.

"Are you dead too?" she asks.

"No." I shake my head. "Of course not." The wind surges, spraying cold water over my face and I taste salt on my lips.

"Then why are you fading?"

TRUTH
AND LIES

I stare at Nina, confused, then look down at my hands. My fingers are translucent, sand and shells clearly visible through them. I turn them, over and over again. This isn't possible. I'm not dead. So why am I fading?

My breath judders into my lungs. I try to run back in the direction of the house, but the sand pulls on my feet so it feels like I'm moving in slow motion.

Thoughts zoom through my mind. Not being allowed past the fence. How the living always seem so warm. The way The Gate felt familiar when I leaned into it. Could I be dead? Is that possible? I remember the way my hands felt weird when I went to the bothy with Benjamin, just like they do now. I look down at my fingers again, and see my feet through them. I dig my nails into my palms but feel nothing.

My hands are cold and numb, that's all. And the fading must be a trick of the moonlight. I squeeze my nails into my palms even harder, until I feel pain. There. I can't be dead. But still my mind swirls. Something isn't right.

"Come on," I shout. "We have to get back." I run closer to the water, where the sand is firmer, and pick up speed. I need Baba. She'll explain this. She'll make everything all right again.

"Slow down!" Nina calls after me, breathless. "What's wrong?"

I can't slow down, and I can't explain. My head is spinning, my vision blurred. My cheeks are hot and wet, although I don't know if it's from tears or the spray off the ocean.

My heartbeat thunders and blood pounds in my ears. A rush of anger burns through me as I realize whatever is going on, it's something Baba has kept from me.

The pounding gets louder, until the whole ground is shaking, and a wave of relief washes over me as

I realize the house is approaching, hurtling towards us through the darkness. Huge chicken feet skid to a halt in a storm of sand and spray and the house leans over me like it wants to scoop me right up.

"Marinka." Baba opens the door as the house lowers to the ground. "I've been so worried." She spots Nina and her face changes; from concern, to realization, to disappointment.

I stare back at her, and hold up my hands. "I faded!" I shout. "Why did I fade?"

Something flashes in Baba's eyes, maybe sadness, or guilt, but she blinks it away before I can figure it out. "We'll talk about that later. Look at this girl!" She turns to Nina. "Goodness, child, we must get you inside." She beckons Nina to the porch steps. "What is your name?"

"I…" Nina bites her lip, tears welling in her eyes. "I don't know." She looks like she's about to disappear completely. She's just a pale green dress, a faint shadow of long dark hair, and big, lost eyes.

"What is her name, Marinka? How long has she been here?" Baba asks.

"Why did I fade?" I shout again, even louder, stamping my foot on the sand. "Am I dead?"

Baba's shoulders fall. "I'll explain soon. Come inside." She wraps her shawl around Nina and ushers her through the door. Already the house is giving Nina energy for her journey, making her seem more real. I inspect my fingers. They are solid again. I press them into my palms and feel my fingernails straight away.

The door swings shut. Baba has gone inside without even answering my question. It's all about the dead and the guiding for her. What about me? Don't I have a right to know what I am and why I'm here, stuck in this stupid house on legs? I kick the porch steps, so hard I make my big toenail bleed. "Argh!" I shout into the empty sky. "I hate this house!"

The house shuffles down into the sand, melts the porch steps towards me, and opens the front door. I turn my back on it and stare at the sea. It's not fair. Baba should have answered me, and explained why I faded. A tear escapes from the corner of my eye.

Jack lands on my shoulder, one of his wings smacking me hard on the ear. "Get off!" I yell, pushing him away. "You're so clumsy!" I fall to my knees in the sand, ashamed of myself. It's not like this is Jack's fault. I put my head in my hands, in the hope it will stop it from spinning, and Jack pushes something soft and wet into my palm.

I open my fingers, look at the squashed fish dumpling and laugh. It's a strange laugh, made of too many emotions I can't control. Jack tilts his head, silver eyes shining in the moonlight, and cackles back at me.

"Come inside, my *pchelka*." Baba's shadow falls over us. I push myself to my feet and wipe my eyes. I don't want her to see me crying. I want her to know how angry I am that she kept this, whatever this is, from me.

Nina is wrapped in Baba's shawl by the fire, a bowl of fresh *ukha* in her hands. She stares at the flames beneath the cauldron, memories dancing in her eyes. She looks slightly more solid than before, but her edges are still drifting into the air. "Will she be all right?" I ask, my stomach twisting.

Baba frowns, drapes my thick horsehair blanket around my shoulders and leads me to a chair at the table. She pours a bowl of *ukha*, passes it to me, and steam rises between us. "Why didn't you tell me she was here?"

I look down at the soup and shrug.

"You know what a serious responsibility guiding is. We're here to help these souls complete their cycle. They can't stay in this world after death. You know that. They'll fade away and be lost for ever."

I push a lump of pale fish around with my spoon, submerging it beneath the stock, and then watching it bob up again. I can't believe Baba is going on about responsibilities and dead souls when she still hasn't answered my question.

Baba shakes her head. "I'm disappointed you kept this from me."

"What about what you kept from me?" I shout. "When were you going to tell me I'm dead?" I stare at her, eyes blazing, willing and wanting her to tell me I'm not dead. I need her to make everything all right again.

Baba sits opposite me and sighs. She opens her mouth to speak, but no words come out. She shuffles in her chair and tries again. "What does it matter that you're dead?" She shrugs stiffly. "You're the next Guardian. I've always told you that."

"It's important to me." Tears pour down my face as the truth seeps in. I'm dead. How can I be dead? I'm not like the faded dead that drift to the house at night. "This doesn't make sense," I say, shaking my head. "I feel alive. I feel real. And you said souls can't stay in this world after death. So how am I here?"

"You're different. You're Yaga, the next Guardian—"

"Are all Yaga dead?" I interrupt, frowning as I try to make sense of it all. "Are you dead too?"

"No. Yaga aren't dead. But it makes no difference that you are." Baba waves my death away like it's no big deal. "You've lived in this house so long it's given you enough energy to seem alive. You can do everything a living person can do, while you're here."

"Then why did I fade?" I ask, although I know the answer already.

"Because you left the house." Baba's eyes well up. "The further you go away from the house, the more you'll fade. You can only exist here, on the threshold of life and death."

I drop my spoon into my bowl and abandon all

pretence of eating. I feel dizzy and sick. How can I live here for ever? If I'm dead, if I can only exist here, in this house, then all hope is lost. This morning at least I had hope of somehow escaping this destiny. But now I realize I am stuck. Stuck in this house on legs, always moving, never making friends. For ever.

"It's not fair!" I shout, so loud it makes my ears hurt. "I don't want to live here and I don't want to be the next Guardian!" My skin is hot, all the muscles in my neck tight.

Baba's face falls and I see sorrow in her eyes. "You can't change what you are, Marinka. You made this choice."

"I never made this choice. This isn't what I want. I want a normal life, and a normal house and a normal grandmother." I regret it as soon as I say it, but I can't take it back, so I just stare at the slowly congealing *ukha* in front of me.

Baba puts her hands on mine. "You died when you were a baby, and I guided you through The Gate. But you came back. Your soul chose to stay here, with me and the house. You must be Yaga."

I lean back in my chair and stare at her. I can't be Yaga. Baba is calm and wise, and she loves this life with the dead. It makes her smile and sing and dance. But I'm not like her. I'm not like her at all. A thought suddenly occurs to me and with it an icy chill rushes through my veins. "You're not my real grandmother, are you?"

Baba squeezes my hands tight. "I love you as much as any real grandmother. More. You're the best thing that ever happened to me."

My jaw drops open. "I don't understand. What about all the things you told me about my parents?" I clutch at the memories Baba gave me of them, and they start to unravel. "Were they all lies?" My voice rises as I realize I have no idea what is true any more. "Are they even dead?"

"Yes. They died in a house fire, as I told you. But you were with them."

The image of a Yaga house in flames runs through my mind, as it has done a thousand times before, but this time I doubt everything about it. "Was it a Yaga house?" I demand. The room is spinning, my whole world falling apart at the seams.

Baba looks at our hands, still entwined on the table, and shakes her head.

"Why would you lie about that?" I pull my hands away and glare at her.

"I'm sorry. I didn't mean to lie or hide the truth. It's just..." She looks up at the rafters, like the words she's searching for are up there. "It's just I loved you being my granddaughter, so your parents being Yaga crept into all the stories I told you about them. As time went on it became more and more difficult to tell you the truth."

"So my parents weren't Yaga?"

Baba shakes her head again and a glimmer of hope sparks in my mind as I realize being Yaga isn't in my blood after all. But it flickers out again when I remember I'm dead, so I'm stuck in the house either way.

"The bones!" I blurt out, scowling at Baba as I remember all the times I've worked with the fence bones, believing it was something my parents had done.

"You wanted something that belonged to your

parents, and you liked being outside." Baba looks at me apologetically. "It made you happy to think the bones were once theirs."

"Is anything true?" I rise to my feet, wanting more than anything to storm off, but there are still so many questions I want answers to, and there is nowhere I can run to anyway. I retreat to the wall and lean against it, my legs all wobbly. My mother sails through my thoughts, paddling over dark, starry waters. "The gondola story," I sob. "It's all lies!"

"No, that wasn't a lie. I guided your parents, so their lives added to mine. All the stories I told you about them were true. They did meet in The Sinking City, just as I said. I only added the bits about their houses being Yaga houses. I wanted us to be a family, not just me and you, but your parents too. I guess I was daydreaming out loud. I always wanted a family of my own."

I look at Baba like I'm seeing her for the first time. As someone who also dreamed of being more than Yaga; of having a family and a life beyond the house with chicken legs.

"Your parents loved you more than anything." Baba dabs her eyes with her shawl. "It was their deepest regret they wouldn't get to watch you grow. They wanted you to live so much. When I guided them I felt all their emotions as if they were my own, so when you came back it brought me so much joy. I knew I could love you as much as they did, and give you a life. Maybe not a life with the living, but a life as Yaga. I know it's not the same, but it can be wonderful if you give it a chance. How many people get to travel the world in a magical house?"

Vines fall from the rafters, tiny white flowers blooming along their length as they curl underneath me, and entwine to make a swing seat. I untangle myself from the house and sit back at the table. "But I don't want to be Yaga." My heart feels like it's cracking into pieces.

Baba reaches for my hands again and looks into my eyes. "You're bound to the house, and the house is bound to The Gate, and the dead must be guided."

I roll my eyes away but Baba squeezes my hands until I look back at her. "You're a good girl, Marinka. So I know you'll care for the house as it cares for you, and I know you'll do the right thing for the dead." A smile spreads across her face. "But you're also clever, stubborn and fiery, so if anyone can figure out how to be Yaga and *more than* Yaga, then it's you."

"But how... What do you mean?"

"We need to guide her through The Gate." Baba tilts her head towards Nina. "Then you can figure it out. Everything will fall into place, I'm sure of it. The morning is wiser than the evening."

I look at Nina, sitting comfortably in front of the fire. "Do we have to guide her now? Can't it wait until tomorrow night?"

Baba shakes her head. "She's been here too long already. Come on." Baba pulls me up. "Help her remember who she was."

I talk to Nina. Call her by her name and remind

her about the white house on the edge of the desert. The channels her father dug, and the seeds he planted. The figs, orange trees, and the oleanders he grew for her mother, because she loved the flowers so much. I remind her about her sisters, and the camel she once had, and the chameleons and cobras she found in her garden.

Her eyes shine as she remembers more. Grandparents visiting, bringing fruits from faraway lands and a small wooden doll with cheeks painted pink. She remembers planting seeds with her father, earth in her fingernails, trees growing tall and filling with life. Sitting with her mother, watching speckled wings and silver eyes fly through sunsets. I'm there with her. I see it all and feel it all.

Nina's happy memories mingle with the sadness I feel at losing my friend and a lump forms in my throat.

The Gate opens. Everything in the room leans towards it. I grip my chair to stop from sliding in. Baba appears at Nina's side. "What do you take with you to the stars?" she asks.

"The joy of nurturing life," Nina replies.

Baba kisses her cheeks and leads her to The Gate, murmuring the death journey words. I watch them walk away, confused. Why didn't Baba let me say the words?

"We carry with us memories of infinite value, the joy of nurturing life." Baba looks back at me and smiles. Tears are in her eyes and I know something is wrong.

"I have to go with her," she whispers. "I'm sorry."

"What? No!" I shoot up, knocking over my chair and crashing into the corner of the table. "You said we should never go into The Gate."

"She's been here too long, she's weak. I must show her the way. Help her over the glassy mountains. Maybe even a little further… You will be fine, Marinka. I have faith in you and the house." Baba nods and steps into the darkness. *"Peace at returning to the stars. The great cycle is complete."*

"No! Wait!" I shove the table out of the way and rush towards her, too late. The Gate blinks out, and just like that I'm all alone.

THE NEXT GUARDIAN

I sit in silence, staring at the space where The Gate was, waiting for Baba to come back. She will come back. She has to. She wouldn't leave me here, all alone.

The house sighs, pulling a draught down the chimney and the candles flicker out. The dying embers of the fire cast thick, rolling shadows across the room. I crawl into Baba's chair and pull my horsehair blanket over me. Baba said the morning is wiser than the evening. Maybe she meant she'll return in the morning and then everything will be all right.

She doesn't, and it's not. The morning brings harsh sunbeams that pour through the skylight and illuminate an empty, silent room. No humming, no singing, no shuffling of feet. Not even the click of Jack's claws or the bleating of Benji.

"Jack!" I shout. My voice cracks and ends in a sob. Jack pokes his head through the skylight and shrieks. Relief washes over me. I'm not completely alone. Jack always comes back, and surely Baba will too.

I carry Benji inside to make the house seem less empty, and busy myself with tidying so that everything will look nice when Baba returns. Benji skids around the floor as I clear away last night's food and dishes and wipe the table. Then I decide Baba will be hungry when she gets back, so I build a fire, make fresh black bread dough and leave it to rise in the warmth.

When she's still not back I go for a walk along the beach, to look for a good spot for us to skinny-dip and sunbathe later. I choose an area with a huge palm bending over it, creating a cool shadow for Baba. She would like it here, in the shade. I gather dry sticks for a campfire and think about what we could cook. We'll have a night off tonight, like Baba wanted to, and spend it together, just the two of us. I get everything ready: food and drink, candles and books, blankets and Baba's *balalaika* so she can play music and sing to the stars.

But when I've prepared it all, she's still not back. A knot forms in my stomach.

The sun dips low in the sky and Jack shouts from the top of a skull. Of course! Baba can't come back until The Gate opens, and that always happens at night. I should have realized that before. I'm not thinking straight. I light the skull candles, but leave the skeleton gate with the foot-bone hinges closed.

As darkness falls, the dead gather by the fence, but I ignore them. I'm not letting them in. I'm not guiding the dead without Baba.

I lay the table with the black bread I baked, salted butter, Circassian cheese, horseradish and *kvass* – all the things that Baba likes best – and I sit and wait for The Gate to open and Baba to return. Benji falls asleep on my floor cushion and Jack dozes in the rafters.

The knot in my stomach tightens as the night

draws on. I hear the restless dead shuffling outside, the occasional murmur and groan of impatience. I pull the shutters closed and latch them tight, but still I hear them. The noise chills me to my bones, because it reminds me I'm one of them. I'm dead too. Technically I don't even have bones to chill.

What am I? A lost soul that wouldn't go through The Gate, only made real, or almost real, by the magic of the house. If I'm only able to exist here, near the house, what kind of life is this?

Memories of the life I've had drift through my mind. Sitting on Baba's lap when I was small, snuggling into her warm belly as she told me stories. Dressing up as a knight and battling stick armies the house grew for me. Bouncing on the roof, held tight by soft, fuzzy vines, as the house splashed through puddle-filled wetlands. Landscapes whizzing past, the house running through the night. Watching flamingos, whales and polar bears from my bedroom window. Dancing with the dead to Baba's accordion, and falling asleep while she played lullabies on her *balalaika*. If I had passed through The Gate as a baby, none of these things would have happened. The life I've had is certainly better than no life at all.

I stare into the fire, guilt weighing me down. So many of the things I've said to Baba I regret now. I don't hate my life, my death, whatever it is. It's been good, growing up with her in this magical house. I need her to come home. Nothing else matters. Whether I'm alive or dead, a Yaga or not, I don't care any more. I just want Baba back.

Jack flops down to the floor and his claws click behind me as I pace the room. "Shhhhhh!" I hiss at him, trying to think what to do. I stop and stare at the space where The Gate always appears. "Gate! Open!" I shout dramatically. Nothing happens.

I try the death journey words, speaking them as loudly and clearly as I can, using Nina's "joy of nurturing life" for the bit that always changes, seeing as that was used the last time The Gate was open. It occurs to me those words are a good fit for Baba's life too. Nurturing brought her happiness, and although she nurtured the dead rather than the living, she always said there was no difference between the two.

The words don't open The Gate though. "House!" I demand, glaring at the rafters, "Make The Gate open!" Nothing happens. I stamp my feet and slump back into Baba's chair.

Jack beats his wings and I lift my arms over my head to protect myself from the collision, thinking he's about to land on my shoulder, but he flies over me and something soft floats down into my arms. I pull it into my lap.

It's Baba's headscarf, the one with the skulls and flowers. It smells of her: lavender water, bread dough, *borsch* and *kvass*. I pull it around me, stare into the fire again, and wait. She has to come back. She just needs a little bit longer. Who knows how high the glassy mountains are, or how long the path to the stars. She'll take Nina as far as she needs to go, and then she'll return and everything will be all right.

Soft knocking breaks me out of my trance. I'm not sure how long I've been staring at the fire but it's nearly burned out and the room is cool. Moonlight pours through the skylight, decorating Jack with a silver sheen. He ruffles his feathers, opens his eyes, and tilts his head towards the front door. I follow his gaze. An old wispy couple are standing in the doorway. I glare at the rafters accusingly. The house had no right to let them through the bone-gate.

"Hello?" the old man says in a wavering voice. "May we come in? My wife is so tired."

I frown as I try to make sense of his words. He's talking in the language of the dead, and I can barely understand him. His wife is hunched over, clutching him tight. Her spine is curved like a shepherd's crook, and she seems unable to lift her head, or stand without his support. I can't send them away like this. I nod reluctantly.

They shuffle to the table and the man helps his wife into a chair. Now they're here I suppose I'll have to guide them away. By myself. Nerves flutter through me. I turn back to the dying fire and fiddle with Baba's headscarf, folding it carefully into smaller and smaller triangles. I'm annoyed with the old couple, for invading my space and for needing to be guided, and also with Baba for not being here to do this. She's Guardian of The Gate, not me.

"Would you like me to mend up your fire?" the old man offers, his hat in his hands and a warm smile on his face.

"No, I'll do it." I throw a handful of sticks onto the embers and they crackle into flames. "Help yourself to food," I add as an afterthought, feeling guilty for being so rude. Baba would be ashamed of me.

"That's very kind." The man reaches for the bread and cuts a couple of thin slices for himself and his wife. "There are more dead out there." He glances to the door.

I edge towards it and push it closed with my foot, ignoring the house's creak of disapproval. "You know you're dead?" I move to the table and sit opposite the old man, intrigued. The dead don't usually realize what they are until Baba tells them.

"Oh yes, we've both been expecting this for some time." He puts his hand over his wife's. "I'm so pleased we'll be making this journey together."

I understand him clearly now. The language of the dead is strange, evading me one minute then making sense the next. I wonder if it's about listening, like

Baba always said, or if it's more about actually wanting to understand. Right now, I realize I want to understand what this man is saying. If for no other reason than it's distracting me from Baba not being here. I pour him and his wife a *kvass*.

"We've been married for seventy-one years," the man says proudly.

"Wow." I can't imagine what so many years feels like.

He looks at his wife fondly. "We've known each other our whole lives. Our parents were neighbours."

"We used to play together as children." The old woman smiles.

They tell me of their lives together; how they sat next to each other at school, got married when they left, and set up a business making clay pots. They tell me about their holidays on the same riverboat every year, and their wish to have children that was never fulfilled. A tear drips from the old woman's face. The old man puts his arm around her, pulls a handkerchief from his pocket and dabs her eyes. I feel a tense, hollow aching deep inside them, caused by wanting something so much for so long. It makes me think of Baba, and all the lies she told because she wanted a family of her own. I wish she were here, so I could tell her I understand now, and I forgive her, and that she will always be my grandmother, no matter what.

The man goes on to tell me how he and his wife gave lessons to children, teaching them to throw clay on a potter's wheel, and how his nieces visited every summer. The couple finish each other's sentences, and hold each other tight. He winks at her, and lights dance in her eyes.

I'm swept away by their words, to a home filled with handmade pots and ornaments. I smell tea, clay and glaze, and hear the laughter of children in lessons. Decades of memories fly by, too fast. Seventy-one years doesn't feel as long as I thought it would. I don't even notice The Gate is open until the man rises to his feet and helps his wife to hers, and they hobble slowly towards it.

"What do you take with you to the stars?" I ask, suddenly remembering my role in all of this, rushing to pour the spirit *trost*.

"The warmth of companionship." The woman smiles and the man nods in agreement. They drink the *trost*, kiss my cheeks, and hold hands as they step through The Gate together.

The death journey words flow from my mouth as they drift into the blackness. *"May you have strength on the long and arduous journey ahead. The stars are calling for you. Move on with gratitude for your time on Earth. Every moment now an eternity. You carry with you memories of infinite value, the warmth of companionship. Peace at returning to the stars. The great cycle is complete."*

I stare after them, searching for Baba. I try to make out the waves that hush below me, try to focus on the faint outline of the glassy mountains. Lights flash like fireflies. I feel myself being pulled towards them.

"Baba!" I shout, but although I feel the words in my throat no sound comes out. My voice is swallowed by the darkness. I lean further into The Gate, see the stars in the distance, above, below and beyond. Baba is in there, somewhere. If I stepped inside I could find

her and bring her home. And then everything would
be all right.

I take a deep breath, pull myself to my full height,
and step calmly into The Gate.

A Painful
Splitting
Sound

BANG!

Something huge and heavy sweeps past my face and lands at my feet. I jump back, look down at the rafter that has fallen from the roof, and then back up at The Gate.

It has disappeared.

"House!" I yell. "I was going to bring Baba home. Open The Gate again."

The house shakes from side to side.

"Please?" I try again. "I can't do this on my own." I put my head in my hands. It feels heavy; weighed down by the memories of the old couple, and Nina, and Serina. "I can't be a Guardian. I have to find Baba."

Two thick vines slap across the space where The Gate was, making a large cross. And just in case I don't get the message, a few tendrils coil up and spell out the word *No* in curly writing right in the centre of the cross.

My whole body stiffens and I struggle to breathe. Once again the house is controlling my life; stopping me from going where I want to go, and preventing me from being with the people I want to be with. I storm through the front door, needing air and space, only to be faced with the dead.

Clouds of them are gathered around the skulls of the fence. Their confused faces turn to me as I step outside, seeking comfort. But I look away and walk around the fence, blowing out the skull candles. As each flame is extinguished the dead drift away, and I sense the house shrink and sag behind me. I feel its disappointment, heavy in the night air.

"It's not like I can guide them," I mutter. "You've shut The Gate."

A wispy old lady steps towards me. "I can't help you," I say before she can ask me anything, and I blow out the candle between us. A crack reverberates through the air. I turn around and peer at the house but can't see where the noise came from.

I blow out another candle, more dead drift away, and there is another crack. Then a creak, and a painful splitting sound. My hands tremble as I move to the last candle. Just as the flame dies I see it. A fracture in the house's wall, near the skeleton store. My eyebrows furrow as I walk towards it. I don't understand. The house has never cracked before. I touch the wood. It feels dry and splintered.

"What's wrong with you?" I whisper, but the house doesn't respond. It's eerily still and silent. Cold shivers through me and I rush back indoors. I stack logs onto the fire until no more will fit and then I sit on the edge of Baba's chair, frowning at the flames. Jack pushes a soggy piece of bread into my sock. I pick him up and hold him close, but I still feel alone.

I need Baba. She would know how to fix the crack. And she would happily guide all the dead that came to the house. She should be here.

If the house won't let me through The Gate, I'll have to find another way to bring Baba home. I rise to my feet and clear the table, and as I put the leftover foods away in the pantry an idea forms in my mind.

I look inside pots and rummage through jars, a small smile tugging at the corners of my mouth. We're getting low on several things: oats and flour, tinned fish and fruits, chilli powder and oil, tea and sugar. And the cold pantry – the section of the pantry the house keeps cool by pulling a draught over damp moss – is practically empty. I pull a piece of paper and a pencil from my apron pocket and write a list.

"Look!" I wave the paper at the rafters triumphantly. "We need to go to the market."

The house sinks lower into the sand.

"Maybe not urgently," I concede. "But we could definitely do with more of these things. Some of them are really important." Benji wakes up and bleats loudly.

"Milk powder, for example! Now that we have Benji the milk powder is going down really fast. And I can't cook as well as Baba. I need more tinned foods and ready-made sauces."

The house adjusts itself with a groan.

"Please," I barter. "Take me to the market and I'll prepare a really big feast. I'll guide a whole army of dead. And I won't try to go into The Gate."

The chimney snorts, sending ashes dancing into the air. The house doesn't believe me.

"Look, I'm sorry." I put a hand on the wall and take a deep breath. "I'm sorry about everything. I know I've been selfish, and I should have guided Nina sooner." My voice breaks as I realize I truly *am* sorry. "It's all my fault." I slide down the wall and collapse onto the floor in a heap. "Baba told me guiding the dead was a serious responsibility but I didn't listen. And now, because of me, Baba has gone through The Gate. I need to get her back and make things right, but I don't know how. Maybe one of the other Yaga can help. Please," I try again. "Take me to the market, so I can find someone to help me bring Baba home."

Tiny blue flowers rise between my fingers and brush against my skin. I'm not sure what that means but I decide to think positive. "Now?" I rise to my feet. "Can we go now? Please?"

The house tilts and I hear a soft splash as its feet rise from the water.

"Thank you." I smile at the rafters, hope and excitement bubbling through me. We haven't been to the market for months. It's a real market, for the living, and one of the biggest street markets in what Baba calls The Land of Origins. All the Yaga go there to get their supplies. It's always busy, street after street filled with traders and shoppers so focused on bargaining and bartering that a house with chicken legs can sneak to the edge without anyone even noticing.

There's a stall that sells the spirit *trost* for the dead. And behind it sits a retired Yaga house, one that doesn't travel the world any more. An Old Yaga lives there, one of the Ancient Elders. She will know how to get Baba out of The Gate, I'm sure of it.

The fence bones clatter into the skeleton store and Benji skids towards me in fright. I lean down to him and he scrambles up into my arms as Jack lands on my shoulder, and I carry them both to the window to watch as the house moves.

My heart surges upwards with the floorboards. Long, slow paces roll into a bounding jog. The house heads north, along the coast. I glance back at the beach where I swam with Nina and though my eyes sting with tears at the thought of everything that happened here, the image of Nina laughing in the surf still makes me smile.

Sandy beach turns into rocky shore and sheer cliff, and then the horizon lights up with the unmistakable glow of a city. Huge dark ships loom out to sea, pinpricks of coloured lights decorating their hulls, and the wind carries the smell of the port: seaweed, fish and people. Real, live, living people.

The market is on the edge of town. From a distance it looks like an inland ocean, the canopies over the stalls billowing like waves. The house slows to a gentle stroll and circles closer. When it's sure it has found a quiet spot, it folds its legs and lowers itself gently to the ground.

I'll never be able to sleep, and it seems Jack is just as excited as me. He squeezes through the gap at the bottom of the window sash, opens his wings wide and flaps majestically into the night. I'm sure the spirit *trost* stall will be open. Baba has visited the Old Yaga who runs that stall at all times of the night. I tie Baba's headscarf under my chin, pull a shawl around my shoulders and, with a deep breath of the spiced air, walk out into the night alone.

THE OLD YAGA

I know the retired house and the Old Yaga's stall is somewhere on the edge of the market, so I weave my way through the makeshift streets in a great circle, checking my hands every few minutes to make sure I'm not fading. Everything is quiet and peaceful, but electricity shivers through the air, like the market is waiting for the living to wake up.

Once I've got Baba back, we'll walk through these streets together while they're filled with living people. She'll barter for old musical instruments and tinned foods, and I'll look at clothes and second-hand books. And instead of being distracted by daydreams, I will hold her hand and appreciate every moment. Not like before.

A wave of cold, damp air breaks my chain of thought. The ground is wet from where a stall must have been washed down. I step over a shining puddle and look up.

"What do you see?" The voice makes me jump. I squint into the darkness, in the direction the words came from. A long curved pipe swings out and points at the puddle. "What do you see?" the voice asks again, and I realize it's talking in the language of the dead. Relief washes over me. A Yaga!

I look at the puddle, confused. It's just a puddle. "Water?" I reply, unsure of myself.

A face appears behind the hand holding the pipe; dark, deeply wrinkled skin and eyes shining with moonlight. It's the Old Yaga who runs the spirit *trost* stall. Part of me wants to rush to her and hug her, because she is something familiar and a chance at bringing Baba home, but I just stand frozen, my head swimming with hopes and doubts.

The Old Yaga chuckles and I frown. I'm not sure why my answer to her puddle question is so funny. She takes a pull on her pipe and exhales a plume of caustic smoke. I hold my breath until the cloud disperses. "It's good to see you, Marinka. Come in." She beckons me through heavy fabric curtains, past tables decorated with skulls and bottle racks filled with spirit *trost*, to the back of her stall, where the gnarled front door of her retired house is hidden.

A picture of a bottle of spirit *trost* has grown over the wood, with raised images of the dead all around it. Most people would mistake them for depictions of the living, but I recognize the signs; the confusion in the faces and the blurring of their edges is visible even in the simple lines.

The door opens slowly with a drawn-out creak, revealing a front room similar to ours. A fire burns brightly in the hearth and the smell of *borsch* hangs in the air. Shining copper pots and pipes are piled up in the corner though, where Baba would keep her musical instruments, and there are old books and papers strewn across the floor in front of a rickety bookshelf.

The Old Yaga offers me a chair and ladles me out a bowl of soup. "You've come because your Baba has passed through The Gate."

"How did you know?" I tilt my head and stare at her. Although she is old, much older than Baba, her hair is thick and black as the night. Just a few tiny coils of white dot her head like stars. She stands tall and proud, and the air of confidence surrounding her makes my nerves tingle.

"I understand the ripples that whisper through The Gates." The Old Yaga sits opposite me, back straight and eyes keen. "It wasn't quite her time, I think."

"No." I look down and poke my *borsch*. "She had to go through The Gate to help guide one of the dead to the stars. She'll be back. Won't she?" I hold my breath as I wait for her response.

"I've only heard of a Yaga returning through The Gate once before." The Old Yaga leans towards me. "Have you heard that story?"

I shake my head and she strides over to the bookshelf, picks up a thick leather file and flicks through the loose pages.

"It's in here somewhere. I was going to put it into the next volume of *Yaga Tales*. Do you read them?"

"Oh, yes." I nod, memories of dawn-lit bedtime

stories flooding my mind. "Baba used to read them to me when I was little."

"I give a new volume to all the Yaga every ten years or so. I'm a few years late with this one. Finding the time to press over a thousand copies is difficult."

"A thousand copies," I whisper. I had no idea there were so many Yaga. I've only ever seen fleeting glimpses of one or two here, at the market. For a moment it feels comforting to know there are so many others, and I begin to imagine what they might be like. But then I push the thoughts away. It's pointless wondering, because I'll never know them. They all lead secret, lonely lives – like me.

The Old Yaga returns to the table with a few yellowing pieces of paper. "Here's the story. Can you read it?"

I glance at the ornately written words and shake my head. "It's in the language of the dead."

"That's not a problem, is it? You've been doing fine this evening. Much better than the last time I saw you."

Heat rises into my cheeks. Baba and the Old Yaga

always spoke in the language of the dead when we visited, so I never paid much attention to their conversations. Looking back, I suppose I should have tried harder to be polite. I look at the words on the paper again and start to read slowly.

"*The Baby Who Would Not Be Guided.*

"*Once, in the days of taller trees and longer summers, a baby came to The Gate, carried on the back of an easterly breeze. She had red hair and a cheery smile and the impatience and temper of a bee in a jar.*"

My eyes widen and I read faster.

"*The Yaga gave her a spoonful of goat's milk, swaddled her in a horsehair blanket, and sang lullabies to soothe her restless soul. As the baby calmed and fell asleep the Yaga kissed her cheeks and sent her through The Gate, as was the custom and her responsibility.*

"*But the baby drifted back.*

"*So the Yaga fed her a spoonful of damson jelly and swaddled her in her own headscarf and sang the songs of old. The baby fell asleep once more and the Yaga kissed her cheeks and sent her through The Gate.*

"*But the baby drifted back.*

"The Yaga, fearful that the baby would fade away, as souls do when they don't return to the stars, took a deep breath to fill her lungs with courage, held the baby tight and stepped into The Gate herself.

"Being heavier than the dead, who float to the stars, she fell into the black ocean. She fought with her arms and legs against the icy waves until they were all twisted by the currents. Still she held the baby tight, and swam all the way to the base of the glassy mountains.

"She could feel the baby pulling, back towards the land of the living, so she held the baby tighter and climbed the sheer cliffs of the glassy mountains using her teeth and nails until they were all crooked with the strain.

"Still the baby pulled back towards the land of the living, so the Yaga held her even closer and carried her further, over the great rainbow and through light years of darkness, until they reached the birthplace of the stars.

"There the Yaga kissed the baby goodbye and let her go, to return to the stars from whence she came. Exhausted and far from the land of the living, the Yaga

did not know if she could make the journey home.

"Each step was a battle against the natural order of the great cycle. The Yaga fought against solar winds and meteor showers, against billowing storm clouds and deep black holes. She pulled herself home along moonbeams, and by the time she reached The Gate she felt a thousand eons old, weighed down by the blackness of the void, but satisfied that she had fulfilled her responsibility to the child.

"But as she stepped across the threshold of the living, she heard a baby cry at her back. She turned around to find the red-haired baby girl holding on tight to her shawl, smiling her cheery smile.

"The Yaga sighed, knowing she could not go into The Gate again, as she was too tired and too old now to make the journey both ways. So she gave in to the child's stubbornness and let her stay, deciding that if the baby would not be guided, she would raise her as a Yaga. Because although not born to be one, as most Yaga are, the child could not go back to the land of the living, and would not go forward to the land of the dead."

I finish the story and put the paper down with trembling fingers. "This is about me, isn't it? About when Baba tried to guide me when I was a baby."

"You were a stubborn little thing." The Old Yaga smiles. "But it worked out well, I think. Your Baba loved you as if you were her own, and it looks like she has raised you to be a fine Yaga. It's a shame she's left early. You're a little young to take over the house and The Gate by yourself, but I'm sure you'll do fine."

"Oh no," I say quickly. "Baba is coming back. The story proves it. She's done it before, so she'll do it again."

The Old Yaga says nothing and her silence pricks at my skin.

"She is coming back." I try to say it more confidently, but my voice wavers. Some of the last words from the story echo through my mind: *she was too tired and too old now to make the journey both ways.*

"How is your house?" the Old Yaga asks.

"It's fine." I dismiss her question, a cold wave of panic rushing through my chest with the realization that Baba might be gone for ever. I bury the thought deep inside, unable to accept it.

"Have you guided any dead on your own yet?"

"No," I lie. "That's Baba's duty."

"And your duty now, if you are the next Guardian. You must start soon, before your house begins to suffer."

"What do you mean, suffer?" I frown as I remember the painful splitting sound when I sent the dead away.

"Yaga houses live for the dead. Guiding is their reason for being. Without it they are lost. They wither away."

I picture the crack that appeared in the house's wall by the skeleton store, with the dry splintered wood all around it, and my stomach tightens.

"And it's not only your house that will suffer. The dead need to be guided. Trapped in this world, they fade away and can be lost, for ever. Some of the other houses may guide more, of course, in an attempt to stop that from happening, but they will suffer from the strain of guiding your share of the dead. It is essential that every house guides, or the whole cycle goes off-balance." The Old Yaga points at me with the end of her pipe and frowns. "And then there is you of course."

"Me?" I croak. My mouth is dry.

"You are linked to your house in a unique way. What will happen to you if your house withers away?"

My gaze darts to my fingers and they tremble as I picture them fading. Nausea rises inside me as I imagine my whole body disappearing, and my soul being lost for ever. I dig my fingernails into my palms just to feel alive.

"So. We need to get you guiding." The Old Yaga raises her eyebrows. "You speak the language of the dead beautifully, when you want to. Do you know the death journey words?"

"Yes. No. Well, sometimes. I mean I only just learned them. I'm not ready." I shake my head. It's still heavy with the memories of the souls I've already guided.

"Nothing like being thrown in the deep end to learn how to swim." The Old Yaga laughs.

I remember the house kicking me off the cliff into the lagoon. I feel like it's happening again; like I'm breaking the surface, gasping for air, desperately reaching for something solid.

"Are you all right?" The Old Yaga's face crinkles

with concern. "Do you want to stay here tonight? I've a spare room made up. We can talk more tomorrow about how you can guide alone."

"I have to get back to the house, and Jack and Benji." I sway as I rise to my feet. My world is falling apart, and the Old Yaga wants to talk about guiding. But I can't. I can't be the next Guardian. There must be a way to bring Baba home so *she* can guide the dead, and protect me and the house from crumbling and fading and the cycle from going off-balance. Being Guardian is her responsibility. Not mine.

"Of course." The Old Yaga walks me to the door. "Come back tomorrow night. I'll help you prepare for your guidings then, if you like."

"Thank you," I hear myself murmur. I watch my arms brush aside the fabric drapes on my way out to the street, and I stumble through the puddle into the light of the early morning. I feel like I'm in an itchy, uncomfortable nightmare, where I can't get enough air, and I can't wake up, no matter how hard I try.

Laughter rises to my left. I look up and see two girls, about my age, watching me from the next stall.

One whispers something to the other and they both giggle.

"Where did you get that headscarf?"

"You look like the ugly witch who lives in that rotten old house."

"It's not mine." I pull the scarf from my head. I was about to say it's my grandmother's, but that's not true any more. How could Baba do this? Leave me here, all alone, in danger of fading away. And expect me to become the next Guardian.

I don't want her scarf. I don't want the scarf of a Yaga. I don't want to look like a Yaga, or be a Yaga. I drop the headscarf into the puddle, skulls and flowers swirling in the muddy water, and I walk away, desperately trying to think of a way out from all of this.

SALMA

I arrive back at the house and stare at the crack near the skeleton store. It looks longer, the area of splintered wood around it even wider. Frustration burns through me. "This is your fault!" I snap. "If you'd let me into The Gate, I could bring Baba home and she would guide the dead and then you'd be fine."

The house sags and shakes slowly from side to side.

"You're so stubborn!" I yell. "Please just…" I shake my head and storm inside. There is no point talking to the house. I know it won't let me through The Gate. Baba said I should never cross the threshold, and the house will back her up. Even now, when me going through The Gate might be the only way of saving all of us.

Jack isn't back yet, but Benji is asleep in my room. I lie down next to him, by the mossy fort, and groan. The Old Yaga was no help. She thinks Baba is gone for ever, I can tell. But there must be a way to bring her home. If I could get through The Gate, maybe I could carry her back, the way she carried me when I was a baby.

I sit up, a bubble of inspiration popping in my mind. My house won't let me through The Gate, but the Old Yaga's house won't have a chance to stop me. I'll go there tomorrow night, ask for help guiding, and as soon as the Old Yaga opens her Gate, I'll jump through it, find Baba and carry her home.

I rest my head back on the soft moss, close my eyes and try to fall asleep, comforted by the hope that tomorrow night I can fix everything. But all around the edges of my mind, I see dead souls fading away and Yaga houses crumbling. And when sleep finally comes, they haunt my dreams too.

Rat-tat-tat!

My eyes spring open.

Rat-tat-tat!

I scramble to my feet, squinting against the bright sunlight pouring through the windows. The sounds of the market thrum in the air. Distant footsteps, living voices. The clatter of pots, rustle of packets and clink of coins.

Rat-tat-tat!

"I'm coming!" I call. It's probably the Old Yaga, checking on me, although I'm not sure why the house wouldn't just let her in. I have to pull the door hard to get it to budge, and when it finally does I realize why the house was so resistant.

It's one of the girls who made fun of my headscarf. A living girl. My eyes widen in disbelief. Nobody living has ever come to the front door of the house before. Then I remember I didn't build the fence last night and I flush with guilt. The feeling doesn't last long though, as I start to wonder how many more encounters with the living I might have had if I hadn't always built the fence like I'd been told. And how many more I might have in the future if I never build it again.

"Hello." The girl bites her lip and looks up at me from beneath a furrowed brow. "I'm Salma. My father said I should come and apologize for making fun of you this morning." She sighs loudly. "He heard what my friend and I said, about you looking like a witch. We were only joking. But I'm sorry. So I brought you this." Salma holds up a bright green silk headscarf. My heart clenches because it reminds me of Nina's dress. I stare at it, speechless. Nobody has ever given me a gift before, except Baba of course. "Because you dropped yours in the puddle," Salma continues, "and because this one will go really well with your hair."

"Thank you." I feel the soft, cool silk between my fingers and think of Nina's dress swirling in the ocean when we swam together. "It's beautiful."

Salma nods. Her gaze drifts over the sagging wooden walls and drooping windows. "Your house is so strange. It looks just like the one next to my father's stall. The old woman said it would – that's how I found you... Is that a lamb?" Salma's eyes light up as Benji skids across the floor behind me. "Can I see it?" she asks eagerly.

I hesitate, knowing I shouldn't let the living into the house, but Salma looks at me with shining eyes and soft dimpled cheeks, and I find myself taking a step back. "Yes, of course." I drape the scarf over the back of a chair and pick up Benji. "Would you like to stroke him?"

Salma smooths the top of Benji's head with a finger and giggles.

A gust of wind huffs down the chimney, blowing a cloud of soot towards Salma. She rushes back, waving a hand in front of her face.

"I'm sorry. The house is old, and..." My heart suddenly races with the thought that Salma might see something she's not supposed to. Like the vines wriggling in the rafters, or the cracked skull waiting to be glued, or *The Book of Yaga* left open on a moss cushion. "I was just about to visit the market," I blurt out, lowering Benji to the floor. He scampers off to my bedroom and I lead Salma back towards the front door. "Could you show me round?" I ask, thinking how it would be nice to get away from the house, and all my worries, for a few hours and explore the market with a living girl.

I sense the walls of the house tense, but that just makes me want to go even more. It's not like I can do anything here anyway. I can't do anything until I bring Baba home tonight. Picking up my new headscarf, I tie it firmly under my chin.

"Not like that." Salma laughs. She reaches up to unpick my knot and her warm, living fingers brush against mine. "There," she says, draping the scarf gently either side of my neck, "much better, although you need a new dress. I could show you some on Aya's stall. She's my sister. Would your parents buy you one?"

"Maybe," I say vaguely. "Hold on." I dash to the pantry and take some of the money Baba keeps in an empty pickling jar. I could buy myself a dress. Something pretty, like the living girls wear, and a new scarf for Baba to surprise her with when she gets back.

I pull the front door closed behind us, ignoring the rattle of bones from the skeleton store and the pleading look from the house's windows, and I follow Salma into the market.

Salma holds my hand and pulls me along crowded paths between rows of stalls. At first I'm worried I'll fade and she'll feel my hand disappear, but I'm soon distracted by the living. There are hundreds of them, young and old, dressed in clothes and hats of every shade and design I could ever have imagined. I try to pretend I'm one of them, just a normal, living girl, out for a walk with a friend.

Everything feels unreal, or somehow more than real, like all the colours and sounds have been made richer. Conical mounds of too-bright spices are piled so high they seem to defy gravity. Shining brass lamps and silverware glint like broken pieces of the sun and moon. A monkey in a waistcoat shrieks from a sea of blue-and-white ceramics, and a snake charmer smiles at me in front of a rainbow of jewelled slippers.

Last time I was here I followed Baba through these streets, carrying basketfuls of supplies. She told me not to draw attention to us, that we had to be wary of the living: "Beware the goat from the front, the horse from the rear, and the living from all sides."

Thinking of Baba brings an ache to my heart and a hollowness to my belly. When she returns, I'll tell her how I walked safely through the market with Salma. Maybe we don't have to be so wary of the living after all. Maybe things can be different for us in the future.

"This is where my sister works." Salma pulls me up to a large stall shaded by long, flowing silks and I'm confronted by a smiling, round lady who looks like an older version of Salma.

"Hello, I'm Aya." Her gaze runs over my apron and old woollen dress and she shakes her head. "You must be roasting in that. I'll make you a cool mint tea while you look around." She disappears out the back and Salma leads me around the stall, picking up dresses and holding them under my chin.

"You have to try this one on." She passes me a long green dress that matches my new headscarf, and once again, I'm reminded of Nina. The fabric is soft and light, and tiny shining beads swirl around the neckline.

"Oh, yes." Aya emerges with a tray of iced mint tea and dates. "That looks like it was made for you."

"It is beautiful." I stare at the dress, unsure. It seems so fragile.

"Go on." Salma nudges me into a changing area. "I'll buy some *chebakia* while you try it on."

By the time Salma returns, I feel like royalty. I'm sipping sweet mint tea while Aya paints my hands with henna. The dress is a cool breeze on my skin, and the beads catch the light like dewdrops.

"You look so different." Salma smiles as she offers me a flower-shaped sesame cookie. "You have to get that dress."

It's easy to go along with Salma's decision. I choose a scarf for Baba too; a black one with huge red flowers and long golden tassels. A smile creeps across my face as I imagine them swaying as she dances with the dead.

I pay for the dress and scarf and am about to bundle up my old clothes to carry home when Salma suggests they are not fit for anything but the fire. My chest tightens, but I shake the feeling away and leave my old clothes with Aya.

The next few hours pass in a magical blur. Buzzing with the energy of the market, I almost forget about Baba being gone, and about being the next Guardian. As well as looking like a different person, I *feel* like a different person. But all too soon the sun sinks below the canopies, throwing deep orange light across the stalls. My heart starts thundering as I realize that I've been away from the house all day. Benji will be starving.

"I have to go," I say, feeling heavy and suffocated by the reality of my life crowding back around me. "Thank you for showing me around today."

"You're welcome." Salma smiles. "I was worried about coming over, but it's been fun. And you look so pretty in your new clothes."

Warmth floods into my cheeks. This morning Salma and her friend thought I looked like an ugly witch, but now she's calling me pretty. It feels good to know that although I'm dead, and sort of a Yaga, at least I can pass for a normal, living girl. While I'm near the house anyway.

"I bet my friend Lamya wouldn't even recognize

you." Salma's eyes light up. "Why don't you come over to my riad tomorrow and we'll see if she does?"

"Riad?" I ask.

"My house. It has a garden in the middle. With a pool." Salma leans close and points to a row of big, colourful houses on the edge of the market. "I live in the pink one. Lamya is coming over after breakfast. Can you come too?"

My mouth drops open. I can't believe I've been invited to a normal house, with living people. It's something I've daydreamed about for as long as I can remember. But how can I possibly go? I have no idea what will happen tonight, or where I'll be tomorrow.

And yet, I can't bring myself to say no. "I will if I can." I nod and smile, then I turn and run back through the streets towards my house. A strange guilty thrill shivers through me, because I can't stop myself from imagining things: if I save Baba from The Gate tonight, she and the house might be so grateful that they'll happily let me visit Salma's riad. Maybe they'll finally realize how much I don't want to be a Guardian, and my whole life will change. I'll still be bound to the house, but maybe I'll get more freedom – to explore beyond the fence, as much as I can, and to make friends with the living, and maybe even shape a future of my own. My smile widens because for the first time since I found out I'm dead, I can picture a future in which I'd be happy.

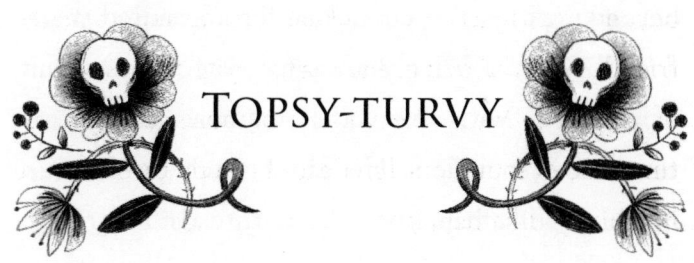

TOPSY-TURVY

I hear Benji's desperate bleats for food before I even see the house. Guilt stabs into my chest and I stumble onto the porch, trying to ignore the scowl of the windows and the splintering mess near the skeleton store.

While I was wandering around the market pretending to be a normal, living girl, Benji was hungry, the house was falling apart, and no one was preparing for a guiding. The great cycle was probably spinning out of control and dead souls were probably fading away. All because of me. The guilty feeling burns into anger and frustration at not being able to have a few hours to myself without everything going wrong.

Benji barges into my shins as soon as I open the

front door, and Jack hurtles towards me, screeching and cawing as if I've been gone for a hundred years. "It's all right!" I lift my arms to protect myself but Jack collides with them and scrambles against my sleeves and shoulders. His claws catch on my new dress and pull at the fine delicate threads. He tries to shove some food into my ear with his beak, but it gets tangled in my new headscarf and I see something red and squishy drip onto the green fabric.

"Get off!" I shove him away as hard as I can. He flaps madly, twists in the air and lands heavily on the floor with a thud. I look down at my headscarf and dress. They're both stained with some kind of red sauce, and there is a ladder on the shoulder of my dress. "Stupid bird!" I yell. "You stupid, clumsy, stupid bird!" I regret the words even as they are flying out of my mouth but it's too late, I can't catch them.

Jack tilts his head; his silver eyes stare at me in shock, then he squawks angrily and struts out of the back door, limping.

"I'm sorry, Jack!" I call after him, but he flaps away without a backwards glance. I pick up Benji and whisper apologies into his ear as I build a fire and hook the kettle over it. He sucks my fingers, crying softly, until the water is warmed. Then I give him a bottle and stroke his soft fur as the milk gurgles down into his belly. Once he's full he falls asleep and I move him onto my floor cushion.

I change into one of my old dresses and leave the new one to soak in a bucket of water. The house is quiet. Too quiet. I go outside and call for Jack but he doesn't come. Not even when I make *kasha* and sit on the porch with a half bowlful just for him, whistling one of his special calls.

The amber glow of sunset fades into a dark blue dusk and I'm about to leave, to go to the Old Yaga's house, when the bones tumble from the skeleton store.

"You want me to build the fence?" I glance up at the porch roof. It nods and I groan. I know the house won't open The Gate in case I go through, so it only wants me to build the fence to keep the living away. It's angry about me going off with Salma today and wants to stop me making friends. "I'll do it when I get back," I snap.

The house creaks as it rises and straightens its legs.

"No!" I yell. "Please! I've got to see the Old Yaga again tonight. She's helping me...she's explaining things; about Baba, and guiding, and..." My heart races. The house can't move on now, not when I'm so close to bringing Baba home. "I'll build the fence when I get back, I promise!"

The windows look at me suspiciously as the house lowers itself back down. The crack near the skeleton store splits further apart and I gasp as I feel a crack in my own heart. Shards of wood fall to the dusty ground and an icy wind seems to blow through my empty veins.

I blink and breathe until the feeling passes, then I pull my shawl tight around my chest and look away from the mess. "I won't be long." My hand lingers on the balustrade as I step off the porch. "Take care of Benji. And keep a lookout for Jack." I swallow back the lump in my throat and remind myself that tonight I'm going to find Baba. And then together we will fix everything.

I run to the Old Yaga's house, push past the curtains, and look at the skulls decorating her stall. They aren't lit for a guiding, but it's nearly dark, so I'm sure they will be soon.

"Marinka." The Old Yaga beckons me inside as her house's door opens. "How are you feeling tonight?"

"Good. Ready to guide the dead."

"How is your house?" she asks.

"Fine." I look at the table, surprised there is only bread and salad laid out. It's not much of a feast for a guiding.

"And Jack?"

"You remember Jack?"

"Of course. When you first brought him here he was just a chick, tucked up in your shawl. You cared for him like a house cares for its Yaga."

"He's more independent these days."

"But you still look after each other, don't you?" The Old Yaga offers me a chair and slices some bread.

I nod, a fresh surge of regret for pushing Jack away twisting inside me.

"Corvids are such clever, sociable birds. When I

was your age I used to watch the ravens and the wolves on The Steppes. The ravens led the wolves to prey, and the wolves let them share their food."

I scoop some salad onto my plate and glance at the door, wondering when the Old Yaga will light the skulls to call the dead.

"They played together too. The ravens pulled the wolves' tails, and the wolves chased them. It took me a while to figure out it was all in good fun." The Old Yaga chuckles. "Do you still play with your house?"

"Pardon?" My gaze swings back to her as I realize she asked me a question.

"Play with your house. Hide-and-seek. Tag. Guide the sole."

The names of the games bring almost forgotten memories to the front of my mind. The house and I used to play hide-and-seek in the forest. That was how I learned the house could climb trees, and creep silently through fallen leaves.

We used to play tag too. I remember running as fast as I could through midnight meadows, the house's feet pounding after me. My heart would thump so hard my whole body shook, and I would scream with excitement until my throat was sore.

When I was too exhausted to run any more, the house would scoop me up with one of its big chicken feet and throw me onto its roof for a piggyback. Holding onto the chimney pot I would bounce up and down until I felt like my lungs might burst from laughing so much.

"I haven't played with the house in years." I push the memories away and sit up straight. "I'm nearly thirteen now." But instead of feeling more grown up, the words make me feel like a lost little child.

"That's a shame." The Old Yaga waves her pipe around the room. "My house and I are both as old as the hills, but we still play together all the time. Maybe not tag." She chuckles. "That would be like a snail chasing a tortoise. But we play tic-tac-toe and...hold tight...TOPSY-TURVY!"

Before I have a chance to grab hold of anything, the whole house falls sideways. Furniture slides across the floor, carrying us with it. My eyes widen in panic and I see the Old Yaga calmly filling her pipe as shelves topple over behind her with an almighty crash.

"What's going on?" I yell, frantically trying to grip the mantelpiece as my chair collides with the wall. Everything that was on the floor is now heaped against the wall and the house is still turning. My stomach lurches as we reach another tipping point and career along the wall towards the ceiling.

"TOPSY-TURVY!" she squeals again, shaking with laughter as she rocks her chair to right herself. I try to do the same but my face is pressed tight against the wall and my legs are trapped under the table. "You have to stay upright as the house rolls over," the Old Yaga shouts.

I smash into the ceiling and end up upside down beneath a jumble of chair legs (technically I suppose it's the house that's upside down, so I wonder if I am, in fact, still the right way up).

"You've lost!" The Old Yaga beams from her chair, which is miraculously the right way up, on the ceiling.

"That's a ridiculous game. Look at the mess." I crawl out from the devastation, hot and flustered, heart pounding. The Old Yaga laughs, which just makes me crosser. I frown and sit on a roof joist, trying to catch my breath.

The Old Yaga lights her pipe and walks to the open window. "Come and see." Leaning out, she points up at the sky. The house's legs are sticking straight up, its toes wiggling in the starlight.

"My house can't walk far or fast these days."
The Old Yaga sighs. "I think soon it will seize up altogether, but it still loves to dance over the Milky Way."

The hairs on the back of my neck lift and a shiver runs down my spine. "What will happen to your house when it can't move any more?"

"Everything is part of the great cycle." The Old Yaga shrugs. "We all return to the stars eventually."

I think of Baba and remember why I'm here. "Shall we get ready to guide the dead now?"

The Old Yaga looks at me out of the corners of her eyes. "My house is old. Ancient. It has guided enough dead in its lifetime to be fulfilled. A younger house took its place as a guiding house many years ago."

"What do you mean?"

"My house is retired. We don't guide the dead any more."

"But you said you'd help me with a guiding!" I gasp, as all my hopes for tonight come crashing down around me.

"I said I'd help you prepare for *your* guidings. I can

help you cook *borsch*, or brew *kvass*, or learn the death journey words."

"I know all that," I snap. "I just need to know how to open and close The Gate by myself."

The Old Yaga sucks on her pipe and nods thoughtfully. "If you bond with your house you'll have more control over your Gate."

"How do I do that?"

"Time, patience." The Old Yaga leads me back across the ceiling and down the walls as her house rolls, slowly and calmly this time, to settle back on its feet.

Frustration boils under my skin. I don't have time or patience. I need to get Baba back now. The house is crumbling and dead souls are fading away, all because of me. "Isn't there another way?" I ask. "Something to help us bond quickly."

"Well, there is the Ceremony of Bonding." The Old Yaga's eyes shine. "I remember our ceremony, when I bonded with this house. It's such a wonderful moment in a Yaga's life. And the party—"

"Party? Ceremony? Baba never told me about any ceremony." I frown. I don't want to feel cross with

Baba again, but she should have told me about this.

"Maybe she was keeping it as a surprise." The Old Yaga shrugs. "It's not like you need to know until it's your time. I have some pictures of the last ceremony I went to." She looks around the room, at her papers scattered across the floor among upturned furniture, and laughs. "I'll have to tidy up a bit to find them. How about I tell you all about it tomorrow night?"

"I could help you clear up now," I offer, eager to find out about the ceremony.

"Oh, don't worry about that." The Old Yaga dismisses the mess with a wave. "You should check on your house, and get some sleep. I'll see you tomorrow."

The door swings open and I'm bundled outside before I can say anything else. The skulls on the stall seem to be silently laughing at me, their mouths twisted into mocking grins. I storm past them and step into the darkness of the market. My skin feels too tight, and I can't shake the feeling I've been tricked, or cheated. I wanted to bring Baba home tonight. What if she is drifting further and further away? What if it is too late already? What if she is gone?

I push the thought away and look up at the sky. It's a deep blue-black, the arc of the Milky Way a brilliant, glittery swoosh of cloud extending across it, from the far east to the far west. Taking a deep breath, I stand tall. It doesn't matter how far away Baba is. I will find a way to bring her home. I have to. Not only to save me and the house, but to save all the dead that are in danger of fading away because they can't get to the stars. I try not to think about all the Yaga houses that are suffering with strain because of me. Everything – the whole of the great cycle – depends on my bringing Baba home.

The house is sleeping when I get back, its eaves slouched and the chimney pot snoring quietly. One of the huge chicken feet is poking out from beneath the porch, and the fence bones are slumped in front of the open skeleton store: a reminder that I promised to build the fence, and what will happen if I don't.

I sigh and shake my head, but kneel down next to the bones and start work. If I don't keep my promise, the house will carry me away in the night, before I get the chance to find out more about the Ceremony of Bonding and how it could help me control The Gate.

Something catches my eye as I lean into the skeleton store to reach one of the long femurs. It's wire, shining silver in the starlight. A long roll of thick ductile wire which I sometimes use to string the bones onto the fence and gate. An idea forms in my mind, shivering with rebellion. I build the fence slowly, letting the idea take root and grow into a plan.

When the fence is finished, built close to the house and covered with sheets and blankets to hide it from curious eyes, I sit on the porch steps and listen to the house breathing to make sure it is still asleep.

One of the huge chicken feet twitches in front of me. The house is dreaming of running. All my life the house has been in control of where we go and how long we stay. But tonight, things are going to change. I creep back to the skeleton store, slip the roll of wire over my shoulder, and begin my task, fingers trembling.

I twist the wire around each of the house's clawed toes, thread it through the spindles of the balustrade, and coil it around the gnarled woody ankle, pulling it as taut as I can. I crawl underneath the porch until I see the other leg, and I manage to weave the wire between three floor joists and wrap it twice around a knee.

Satisfied the house will not be able to stand, let alone walk, I emerge from the tangle of wood, wire and chicken legs with a huge smile on my face. Tonight, for the first time in my life, I will fall asleep knowing that tomorrow I will wake up in the same place.

THE RIAD

I don't sleep as well as I thought I would. The house groans and creaks in the night. It shifts uncomfortably and Benji slides across the floor, bleating in confusion. I bury my head beneath my pillow, and try to ignore the sounds of the crack widening, the wall splintering, and the scrape of wooden legs against wire. I tell myself the house will be fine. And the unguided dead will be fine. And the great cycle won't fall apart because of me. But it doesn't help. Guilt and worries swell and roll through my stomach like a heaving ocean.

In the morning I pretend I can't see the sadness in the skylights, or the disappointment in the rafters. I busy myself feeding Benji, and looking for Jack, who didn't come home last night. I call to him from every window, but he doesn't return. The air seems thick and hard to breathe, and I feel like a great weight is on my chest. I need to escape.

My new dress and scarf are drying in front of the hearth and I remember Salma's invitation to her riad today. It would be the perfect distraction until I go to see the Old Yaga again tonight. I inspect the damage to my dress. The stains are gone, but the shoulder needs stitching.

Baba's sewing box is in her bedroom. Her bed is neatly made, her nightgown folded and placed on the corner with one of her romance novels tucked underneath it. I remember the first time I found one of Baba's books and asked to read it. Her cheeks blushed pink as she told me it wasn't really a story for children. The memory makes me smile, but it makes me sad too. It means so much more now that I know Baba wanted a family. She must have wanted some romance in her life too. Perhaps she was lonely, like me.

I kneel down and slide the sewing box out from under the dressing table. A picture frame topples onto my head and I pick it up. I find myself stroking the face in the photograph with my thumb. It's Baba, holding me as a baby. Her smile is huge, her eyes filled with pride. Emotions rush through me: longing, sadness, guilt, hope, and then anger, hot and tense.

I'm angry with myself for keeping Nina from The Gate, but I'm angry with Baba too. Why did she choose to help Nina instead of staying with me? Was guiding the dead more important to her than being my grandmother?

I slam the picture face-down on the table and storm out of the bedroom, taking the sewing box with me.

My hands tremble as I fix my dress. They are still shaking as I walk away from the house, and I squeeze them together, worried I will fade and be blown away on the back of a breeze. But I arrive at Salma's riad as the sun peaks in the sky, still intact. With a sigh of relief, I lift the huge iron ring on the ornately carved door and knock twice.

A maid opens the door and leads me through a cool, dark room, into an enormous courtyard where the sun blazes down. The floor is covered with tiny multicoloured tiles in intricate patterns. Steps lead down into a deep oval pool, and a fountain sprays mist into the air behind it.

"Marinka," Salma calls. "Come in for a swim."

I gaze at the water, tinted a bright cobalt blue by the tiles beneath it. "I don't have a costume."

"Lamya, can she borrow yours, seeing as you're not swimming?" Salma turns to a girl lying on a low wooden bed and I recognize her from when she and Salma made fun of me.

Lamya reaches into her bag and throws a yellow swimming costume over to me.

I thank her and look around for somewhere to change.

"Do you recognize Marinka?" Salma asks Lamya, her dimples deepening as she smiles.

Lamya looks up at me and shakes her head. "No, should I?"

"She's the girl in the headscarf; the one who visited the old lady next to my father's stall."

Lamya's eyes widen in shock. "The witchy girl?"

"Not witchy now." Salma smiles triumphantly. "I took her to Aya's stall."

Hot and flustered, embarrassed by the girls' conversation and the fact there is nowhere private to change, I wriggle into the swimming costume underneath my dress.

Salma rests her elbows on the side of the pool and peers at my shoulder, a deep frown falling over her face.

My heart races as I follow her gaze. The thought that a part of me might have faded or disappeared altogether is terrifying.

"Is that a tear?" She asks.

I breathe a sigh of relief. My body is fine. It's only my dress that is torn. "My jackdaw caught it with his claws. I tried to fix it, but I'm not very good at sewing."

"Your jackdaw?" Lamya's lips curl downwards. "You have a pet jackdaw?"

I nod. "I raised him from a chick."

"Ugly birds." Lamya pulls a small pot out of her bag and begins painting orange swirls onto her fingernails with a fine brush. "Greedy, and always making tuneless, angry noises. Songbirds make much nicer pets. Have you seen Salma's canaries?"

I glance at the colourful birds in a domed cage in the corner. "They're lovely." My jaw clenches. I don't want to disagree with Lamya, but she doesn't know what she's talking about. Jackdaws are beautiful, generous and clever enough to communicate with a thousand different sounds. And I don't need to keep Jack in a cage for him to stay with me. My heart aches as I think of him. I need him to come back soon.

"You're so pale and thin." Salma stares at my legs as I step out of my dress.

"Like a skeleton." Lamya sniggers.

My chest tightens and I struggle to breathe. Lamya is too close to the truth.

"That's not nice, Lamya." Salma splashes water at her. "Ignore her, Marinka. She's been in a bad mood all morning."

"You started it," Lamya grumbles, leaning back and closing her eyes against the sunlight.

Salma rolls her eyes. "Come on, Marinka. Bring

that ball in with you." She nods to a huge stripy ball in the corner.

I carry it to the pool and lower my legs into the water, unable to see them as anything other than skeleton bones now. The water is perfect though, cool and refreshing, and makes me feel a little better. "Ready?" I ask, holding the ball up to throw to Salma.

We play catch, then take turns seeing who can swim down the deepest while holding the ball. Neither of us can get very far, so we just end up laughing. I beat her in a race when we swim like frogs, but she beats me using front crawl. Out of breath, we float on our backs and look up at the sky. A stork flies down to the pool, spots us and flies off again. Salma tells me they sometimes come to visit the pool in the evening and she chases them off because of the mess they make.

The maid brings us sweet, fruity drinks and *beghrir*, a kind of spongy pancake soaked in honey. After she's eaten, Lamya seems happier, and she offers to paint my nails to match hers. She comments on the shortness of my nails and the roughness of my hands, but gives me some scented cream she says will soften my skin. I think she's trying to be nice.

It's strange spending time with the girls. I don't understand everything they talk about, and I don't feel like I fit in at all, but I think I could figure them out, given enough time. And I want to. I've spent so much of my life dreaming of this, now that I'm finally with the living I want to find out what they do, and understand how they make friends.

"Why were you visiting the old witch in the market?" Lamya asks suddenly, shattering my thoughts of friendship.

"She's not a witch." I pull my hands away from Lamya's

sick.

." Salma nods, popping

says she eats them."

Salma giggles. "That's why he's a storyteller, Lamya."

"There's always truth in stories." Lamya leans forward and whispers, "My grandmother says she feels dark magic around that house and you know she has the gift, Salma."

I curl inwards. I've heard things like this before. Sometimes, when our house has settled within reach of villages or towns, small groups of the living have wandered close to the fence. Adults have hurried away, making strange hand gestures as if to protect themselves. Children have dared each other to creep closer, to try and catch a glimpse of Baba.

Only they didn't call her Baba. They called her cruel names, and said she did horrible things. I don't understand why the living make up lies about the Yaga, and I don't understand why they're scared. It's so stupid. One day they'll need a Yaga, and then they'll be welcomed. I frown as I think of the dead that need guiding. The thought of even one of them fading away because of me makes me feel sic█

"The old woman is strang█ another piece of *beghrir* into her mouth.

"What does she sell anyway?" Lamya asks. "And why do all her customers look witchy, like her?"

"Traditional drinks." I sigh. "And lots of her customers wear traditional clothes. She's not a witch, and she's not strange." I pick up my dress and start to get changed, the feeling that I don't belong here threatening to overwhelm me.

Salma blows on her nails and jumps up. "It's cooler now. We'll walk you home."

"You don't have to do that," I say, not wanting the girls to see the house. I covered up the tangle of wire and chicken legs with sheets, but it looks suspicious and I'm sure Salma or Lamya would ask questions.

"It's fine." Salma smiles. "I said I'd help father pack up anyway."

I reluctantly agree to walk with the girls as far as Salma's father's stall, but say I'll be fine on my own from there. What Lamya said about the Old Yaga has left me feeling tired and bitter. I just want to go home.

The sun is low in the sky, dust and spices dancing in the air. Traders are clearing away their goods and tiny children are begging for unsold food from the stalls. Salma ignores them, and Lamya looks down her nose at them in disgust.

"Urgh, it's Ratty," Lamya says, as she spots a small boy not far from Salma's father's stall. "Go away!" she shouts. "I've told you before about begging round here."

"I'm not begging," the boy protests. "Akram said if I helped him clear away, he'd give me some *bessara*."

"I don't care what you're doing," Lamya snaps. "Just don't do it near me. You smell like a dirty street rat."

Salma giggles and steps around the boy. As she does so, she nudges him sharply with her elbow and he falls to the floor. The boy glares up at her, face red and frowning. "He looks like a rat too, doesn't he?" Salma links arms with me and whispers into my ear, loudly enough for the boy to hear. "Big ears, beady eyes, and goofy front teeth."

I don't say anything, but I wish the ground would swallow me up. Why would Salma be so cruel? Looking up, I notice the Old Yaga watching us from the shadows of the dark curtains around her stall. I turn away in shame, and when I glance back she's gone.

"I really have to go." I pull away from Salma. "Thank you for today." I try to smile but I feel sick.

"I'll call for you tomorrow," Salma shouts after me and my stomach lurches. I don't understand why the girls seem to want to be nice to me, yet then be so mean to others. Pushing that boy was an awful thing to do. And they said cruel things about Jack and the Old Yaga when they don't even know them. After so long wanting to make friends with the living, now I'm not sure I like them at all.

The disappointment feels like a weight on my shoulders. I walk back to the house, legs tired and heavy, feeling even more alone than I did this morning. I don't think things can get any worse...but then I see the house and realize they already have.

THE EXPANDING UNIVERSE

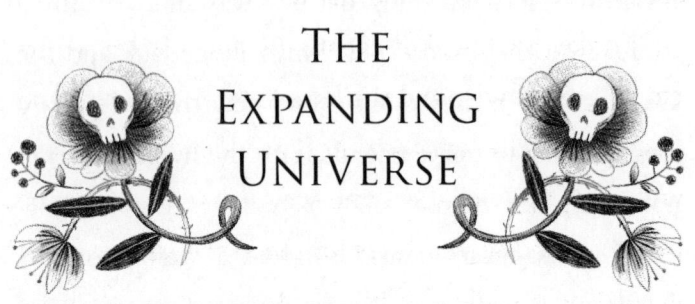

I stare at the mess, a knife twisting in my stomach and my breath coming in short, ragged gasps. Bones from the fence are strewn across the ground, covered in dust and mud. The porch spindles are cracked and broken, the foundations bent at an odd angle. The house has been struggling to get free and, worst of all, the wire has sliced down into the chicken legs, splitting and splintering the wood.

Hot tears run down my face as I scramble around trying to untangle the wire. "I'm sorry, I'm so sorry," I hear myself sob as I attempt to pull the wire away from the toes and ankle. But it's sunk in too deep, and a wide gash on one of the ankles is filled with blood-red sap. I give up and rummage through the skeleton store until I find the wire cutters.

It takes a while, but eventually I'm surrounded by cut lengths of wire and the house is free. I inspect the damage, unsure what to do. I wonder if the house will heal itself, in the same way it has grown seats, play-forts and secret doors for me in the past. Or will it need help to heal? Guilt tightens my throat. Baba believed I would care for the house, but look what I've done. The house has never been so hurt.

Jack lands on my shoulder, his wing hitting my ear and his claws digging into my dress. "Oh, Jack." I reach up to kiss him and stroke his neck. "I'm so glad you're here. I'm sorry about before." He pushes something dry and scratchy into my ear and I take it. A huge crushed beetle. "Thank you." I smile, brushing fresh tears from my face. I try to slip the beetle into my pocket, but my new dress doesn't have any. Suddenly I miss my apron, my old comfy dress and Baba's headscarf.

"Come on." I tap my arm and Jack staggers clumsily down to my elbow. "Let's get the house fixed up."

I pour buckets of water over the wounds, and wrap

torn bed sheets around the two areas that are weeping sap – an ankle on one leg and a knee on the other. The house is tense and unmoving, although at one point it flinches away from my touch, knocking me onto my bottom, and I'm sure that, just at the moment I fall, it shakes with laughter before stifling it. The worry knotted in my belly loosens slightly with the thought that the house might be all right.

When I'm content the wounds are clean and dressed, I clear up the cut wire and neatly stack the bones back into the skeleton store. I don't have time to rebuild the fence, as I must visit the Old Yaga tonight, but I promise myself I'll do it when I get back.

I build a fire and warm some water for Benji's milk. He jumps and skids around the floor until he's eaten, then curls up on my floor cushion at the foot of Baba's chair and falls asleep. Jack stays on my shoulder. I pass him beakfuls of stewed meat from a tin of *tushonka* and tell him everything that has happened since he left.

He listens quietly as I confess to tying up the house, and visiting the Old Yaga to try to get through

The Gate at her house. When I tell him about her house rolling upside down I find myself laughing, even though it made me cross at the time, and Jack cackles into my ear in return.

I try to explain about the girls in the riad; how it was fun playing in the pool, and interesting listening to them talk, but also confusing because although they were mostly nice they also said hurtful, cruel things. I tell Jack that Lamya thinks the Old Yaga is a sinister witch, and that Salma pushed a boy to the ground in the market.

Jack squawks and I remember how I pushed him to the floor and called him names, and how I have hurt the house by tying it up. I sigh, trying to ignore the sickening feeling that I have been just as mean as the girls.

Finally I whisper to Jack about the Ceremony of Bonding, and how it might give me a way to control The Gate. Then I place him on Baba's chair with my horsehair blanket and ask him to watch the house, and Benji, while I visit the Old Yaga. He nods and pushes his beak into my hand for a moment, before turning around and burrowing under the blanket to fall asleep.

My new green dress is torn and stained from scrambling on the floor untangling the house and feeding Benji and Jack, but I don't care. I change into one of my old woollen dresses and feel more like myself as I head out into the night.

The house looks a little better already. The porch steps have realigned and the balustrade is creaking quietly as it bends back into place. Some of the broken spindles are knitting back together and the gashes on the legs don't seem quite as bad as before. I check the dressings, and although the wounds under them are still quite deep they aren't oozing sap any more.

But the crack near the skeleton store is worse than ever. A huge area of wood around it is dry and crumbling. I kneel down next to it and frown. "Why can't you fix this?" I whisper, pressing a hand over my heart in an effort to stop it from aching.

The house doesn't respond, but I know the answer anyway. It's been four nights since Baba held a proper guiding – and the house needs someone to guide the dead. I swallow back the lump in my throat and tell myself that it doesn't have to be me. "I will bring Baba home," I murmur under my breath, and I walk to the Old Yaga's house determined to find a way to open The Gate and bring her back – before the house or anything else gets worse.

It's dark, and the air is warm and sweet with smells from the recently closed food stalls. The skulls outside the Old Yaga's house seem to welcome me with friendly smiles this evening, and the front door opens ahead of me, throwing a glowing rectangle of firelight into the night air.

"Milk soup with noodles?" the Old Yaga asks, putting two bowlfuls on the table before I even get a chance to answer.

"Thank you." I nod and sit opposite her. The house is immaculate, with no sign of the chaos caused by last night's topsy-turvying. Even the bookshelves are tidy, and I notice the Old Yaga has brought a photograph album to the table. "Did you find a picture of a Ceremony of Bonding?" I ask, a shiver of anticipation running through me.

The Old Yaga nods, her eyes sparkling. She looks as excited as I feel as she opens the book and turns it towards me. "This is the most recent Ceremony of Bonding there has been. It was for a young Yaga called Natalya." There is a large black-and-white photograph in the centre of the page. Underneath it, written in faded ink, are the words *Yaga Natalya and her house, Ceremony of Bonding.*

Scores of Yaga are stood in a group, looking directly into the camera with serious expressions. At least fifteen Yaga houses are visible in the background; some poised regally, others balanced on one leg, and two in a blur, like they jumped at the wrong moment. The house in the middle is decorated with garlands of flowers and a young girl is on its porch, smiling.

"I've never seen so many Yaga in one place." I stare at the photograph, breathless. "Baba never told me you gathered together for ceremonies." A frown falls over my face as I wonder why Baba never took me to a gathering. Maybe I wouldn't have felt so lonely if I had known more Yaga.

"Your Baba probably didn't want you getting excited about something that doesn't happen very often. There can be decades, centuries even, between ceremonies." The Old Yaga points at one of the faces in the photograph. "There is your Baba." She slides her finger across to another face. "That's me." Then she taps one of the blurry houses. "And this one is your house, I think."

I peer at the faces she pointed out and recognize both Baba and the Old Yaga. Then I notice a date scribbled in the top corner of the photograph. "How can this be nearly one hundred years ago?" I ask. "That doesn't make any sense."

"Yaga can live for hundreds of years, thousands even, because our houses give us energy, a bit like they give the dead energy to help them on their journey."

I look back down at the photograph and anger churns in my belly. Baba should have told me all this.

"Your Baba told you what you needed to know at the time." The Old Yaga seems to read my mind. "And she must have known you were clever enough to find out the rest for yourself when you needed to."

"How old is Baba?" I ask, another thought edging its way into my mind.

The Old Yaga shrugs. "About five hundred or so."

"So quite young for a Yaga then?" I smile. If Baba is still young, it seems even more likely that I will be able to bring her home.

"There are Yaga many years older than your Baba." The Old Yaga nods slowly. "But, as you will know from guiding, people of all ages pass through The Gate."

"How long will I live?" I ask without thinking, then realize what a strange question it is, because I'm not even alive.

"No one knows how long they're here for."

"I know that," I say impatiently. "But if I live in a Yaga house, like a Yaga, could I be here for hundreds of years too?" The thought is both exciting and terrifying. Hundreds of years to fill with adventures, but hundreds of years of loneliness too.

"It's possible." The Old Yaga tilts her head and smiles. "You're not quite like other Yaga though, are you?"

"Because I'm dead?" The words feel sharp in my throat.

"Well, yes, there is that." The Old Yaga chuckles. "But more importantly, you weren't born to be Yaga. You have a choice."

"What choice do I have?" I scoff. "I can only exist in the house, so what else can I be?"

"What would you like to be?"

"I-I-I want to be a Guardian," I lie, hot and flustered. There's no point talking about what I would like to be. Right now, all I want is to find out how to bond with the house, make it open The Gate, and bring Baba home. Then she can do the guiding and the house will stop crumbling and everything will be all right again. If there *is* a chance I can be something other than a Guardian, I won't be able to figure that out until Baba is home.

"At a Ceremony of Bonding" – the Old Yaga turns back to the photograph but keeps looking at me out of the corners of her eyes – "a Yaga promises to be the Guardian of his or her house, and its Gate, for all their time on Earth. It's a celebration of a bond that can last hundreds, possibly thousands, of years. Are you sure you're ready for that?"

"Of course." My voice is much higher than it should be. I pick up my spoon and slowly take a sip of soup, trying my best to look calm. It's not like I would really be bonding with my house for hundreds of years, I tell myself. Once I bring Baba home, she will take over as Guardian again. "So does The Gate open at the ceremony?" I ask, looking at my soup.

The Old Yaga nods. "Yes. You would have to make your promise to the house and The Gate, with the stars as your witness. There are some traditional words you can learn, or you can make up your own, as long as you promise to protect the house and The Gate, and guide the dead."

"I'll make up my own," I say quickly, thinking that if I jump into The Gate as soon as it opens I won't have to say any words, or make any promises I don't want to keep.

"You really want to do this?" The Old Yaga raises her eyebrows.

"Yes." I sit up straight and look into her eyes.

"As soon as possible. Tomorrow night?"

The Old Yaga hesitates for a moment, then laughs loudly. "Why not? I love a good party, and it's been far too long since we had one. Where would you like your ceremony?"

"What do you mean?"

"Well, we can't have the ceremony here in the market. It's too close to the living. We'll have to go somewhere quiet." She looks up at the rafters and sighs. "It's such a shame my house won't be able to come. It always loved a party."

"Isn't there anything you can do to help it walk again?"

"I'm afraid not. Old age can be cruel. But it's also a blessing, being given the opportunity to live so long." She blows a kiss over to the hearth. "You'll be fine without me for one night, won't you?"

The house rolls its floorboards and shuffles down into the ground.

"That's settled then. Now. Your house can run, so where do you want to go?"

"I don't know. Not too far away." I bite my lip,

remembering my house's injured legs. I hope they are healed by tomorrow night.

"I've always loved The Steppes," the Old Yaga suggests with a wink, "but we could go anywhere. You choose, and I'll arrange the gathering."

"How?" I ask, curious.

"I'll send some whispers through The Gate."

"Oh." I spin around, looking for where The Gate might appear. "You said your house is retired, so I assumed your Gate would be closed for good."

"It's only a tiny window now. Still big enough to hear the whispers though. I'll open it after you've left." The Old Yaga looks at me rather pointedly and I wonder for a moment if she suspected my plan to jump into her Gate.

"The Steppes will be fine," I say, wanting to change the subject.

"Excellent." The Old Yaga smiles.

Warmth surges round my body, and my brain buzzes with thoughts of tomorrow. A gathering of Yaga!

I wonder how many I'll meet and my nerves tingle. Meeting people can bring good things, like meeting

Benjamin gave me the courage to step over the fence and follow my dreams. But meeting people can be difficult too. When I met Nina I made some selfish decisions that led me to lose Baba. And meeting Salma and Lamya showed me that the living aren't always as nice as I thought they would be. I need to be careful. But tomorrow I'm not sneaking around meeting people I shouldn't. I am meeting Yaga.

Always daydreaming about the world of the living, I've never even considered there is a world of Yaga to explore. The universe seems to expand around me. Tomorrow, as well as bringing Baba home, maybe I'll discover new things about the Yaga, and myself. Maybe my future has more possibilities than I have ever imagined.

SHARP WORDS

I drift home on a cloud of hope, and fall asleep dreaming of Yaga houses dancing as Baba plays her accordion. The Gate is open and all the unguided dead are smiling as they drift to the stars. Then my house jumps through the air in a blur, like in the Old Yaga's photograph. But it stumbles and falls and the gash on its knee opens up and pours blood-red sap onto the ground. I wake with a start, shivering with a cold sweat. The house is meant to be running to The Steppes tonight, but it still has bandages wrapped around its legs.

My muscles tense as I open the front door and step onto the porch. But the balustrades don't look too bad. Some of the spindles are a little bumpy and twisted, but they are all in one piece. I climb down to the legs and look at them closely, my muscles slowly relaxing. All the cuts have healed. Only the deep gashes left to inspect.

As I unwrap the bandages, the legs creak and stretch. There are scars, but they are nowhere near as bad as last night. "Would you like to come to a party tonight?" I whisper. "A Ceremony of Bonding on The Steppes. For me and you."

The house leans towards me, opens its front windows wide and stares right into my eyes. I laugh. I've never seen it looked so shocked. "Is that a yes?" I ask. "Will you be able to run?"

With a little shake, the house straightens itself out – until, apart from the crumbling crack near the skeleton store, it is stood as tall and strong as I have ever seen it.

"Good." I run my hand over the balustrade. "You'd better tuck your legs back in then, until tonight."

The house folds its legs underneath the porch and I go inside to make some milk for Benji, and *kasha* for me and Jack.

As I'm clearing away the dishes, there is a knock on the door. I freeze, realizing it will be Salma. She said she would call on me today, and I forgot to rebuild the fence last night. If I had, she might not have come, as the fence has a way of making the living move on. I think about not answering the door but she keeps on knocking, so I decide to open it and tell her I have other things to do.

"Good morning." Salma smiles at me from the steps. "Me and Lamya are going to get ice cream. Would you like to come?"

"No, thank you." I tuck my hands into my apron pocket and find the list I wrote when I was convincing the house to bring me to the market. "I need to buy some supplies."

"I'll help you." Salma tilts her head to look at the list in my hands. "Ali sells most of these things, and I can get his son to deliver them here."

I hesitate. It would be nice to restock the pantry without having to carrying heavy baskets on my own. But I keep thinking of how cruel Salma and Lamya were to the boy in the market yesterday.

"Is something wrong?" Salma's brow crinkles.

"That boy, near your father's stall…"

"Ratty?" She laughs. "Oh, don't worry about him! He won't bother us."

"No, it's not that, it's just…don't you think you were mean to him? Pushing him over like that."

Salma opens her mouth wide in shock. "Me? Mean to him? Oh, you don't know him, Marinka. He's awful. A beggar and a thief. People like that, if you're nice to them, they don't leave you alone. You have to be mean to them. It's the way things are around here."

I look at her, unconvinced. Baba was nice to everyone who came to the house. Rich or poor, beautiful or plain, smelling of roses or dirt. She gave them all food, guided them all with the same amount of care, and they all left through the same Gate.

"Believe me." Salma holds my hands and her warmth flows into me. "I wouldn't be mean to anyone without good reason. Now, where is your dress?"

"I'm wearing this today." I pull my hands away and look down at my apron self-consciously.

Salma wrinkles her nose. "Well, I guess it doesn't

look that bad on you. Kind of rustic. Oh! You know what would go really well with it?" She rummages in her pretty, beaded bag. "This." She pulls out a leather necklace with a wooden pendant carved in the shape of a canary. Tiny flecks of brass are inlaid in the wood to highlight the wings, beak and eyes. "You can have it." She lowers it over my head. "It suits you better than it does me anyway."

I stroke the soft, smooth wood. "Thank you." I still feel uneasy, but it does seem like Salma is trying to be nice.

Jack struts across the floor, his feathers ruffling and claws clicking in agitation. Salma eyes him suspiciously and takes a step back. "Come on." She pulls at my arm. "Let's go and buy your supplies."

It's easier to go along with Salma than argue, and I do want to make sure the pantry is well-stocked, because the Old Yaga said she would help me cook some dishes to bring to the ceremony tonight.

Salma leads me through the market to a huge food stall and haggles with an old bearded man while I drink the sweet mint tea one of his assistants brings me.

"All done," she announces with a smile. "Ali's son will deliver everything to you this evening. You can pay then."

"Really?" I smile. Last time I came here with Baba we had to make trip after trip, carrying baskets loaded with jars. Salma has made everything so easy.

"Yes. Let's go find Lamya and get ice cream."

It's hot and humid now the sun is high. An ice cream would be nice, and I decide it would be polite to buy one for Salma as a thank you for her help.

We pick up Lamya from Aya's stall and wander through the market, licking our ice creams. I've only had ice cream a couple of times before, and never the flavour I've chosen today – lemon. It's delicious, and as refreshing as a cool summer breeze.

The streets are bustling with colour and life. Fabric billows around stalls, cart wheels rumble and a donkey brays. A bamboo flute sings in the distance and the living laugh. Salma and Lamya are happy and smiling, and my heart lifts with the hope that I was wrong about them. Maybe I misunderstood the things they said and did; maybe they aren't cruel or mean after all.

We walk to a tall, round building with a domed roof on the edge of the market, climb a spiral staircase, and sit in the shade at the top of the tower, looking out over the stalls. Most are hidden by the patchwork of multicoloured canopies, but Lamya manages to point out Aya's stall, Salma's father's stall, and the Old Yaga's house peeking out from behind her spirit *trost* stall.

"It looks creepy, doesn't it?" Lamya shudders. "All old and dark and rotten."

My heart plummets through my chest and I rise to my feet, deciding to leave before Lamya starts going on about the Old Yaga again. I don't want her sharp, sneering words to spoil my last day here. After tonight, I don't know when I'll be back in the market.

"Marinka's house is just like the old woman's." Salma licks her ice cream and turns to look in the direction of my house, but it is hidden behind a long red building draped with rugs.

"Really?" Lamya recoils away from me. Then she shakes her head and laughs. "No, Marinka's house can't possibly be as ugly as the old witch's."

"It is." Salma nods. She carries on licking her ice cream, seemingly unaware that her words are hitting me like stones. "Isn't it, Marinka?"

"Neither of our houses are ugly!" I snap, heat flaring up the back of my neck. "You don't know what you're talking about!" My voice keeps rising, and my face gets hotter. I want to stop shouting, but it's like a dam has burst in my throat and the words keep flooding out. "You have no idea what is beautiful or ugly. And you're hateful and cruel. Both of you!"

Salma's eyes pop open in shock. "But I've been nice to you!"

"You haven't been nice!" I yell, pulling the caged-bird pendant from my neck and throwing it onto the floor at Salma's feet. "You tried to turn me into something I'm not."

"I only helped you buy a new dress." Salma's face crumples in confusion. "I thought you liked it."

My breath catches in my throat as I realize this isn't all Salma's fault. I *wanted* to be something I'm not. I wanted to be living, like Salma. So I happily went along with everything she suggested. I wish I had been stronger in myself, and stood up for Jack and the Old Yaga when Lamya said cruel things about them, and stood up for that boy in the market too.

Lamya lifts her chin and looks down her nose at me. "Salma has tried to help you look like a normal girl, instead of the ugly witch-child that you are."

"I'm not a witch!" My eyes burn and my fists clench.

Lamya laughs, although it's not a nice, genuine laugh. It's a laugh that makes my skin crawl.

"Lamya's only joking." Salma reaches for my hand. "And I only meant your house looks like the old woman's. Which it does. Come on, let's go and show Lamya. Then she'll see your house isn't creepy or scary, even though it looks strange."

"Stay away from my house!" The words burst from my mouth, taking me by surprise. But the thought of the girls snooping around my house, judging it and saying hurtful things, is too much to bear. Baba was right. The house needs to be protected from the living. "And stay away from me, too!" I run down the spiral staircase, a storm cloud swirling in my mind. It feels like the bigger my universe grows, the darker it gets. And without Baba here, and with the house cracking apart, I don't know where I can go to feel safe and protected from the darkness.

SPARKS OF LIGHT

I find myself at the Old Yaga's house, stiff and tense from holding back tears. The door opens ahead of me, but the Old Yaga isn't in her front room. I collapse onto a chair by the fire, close my eyes, breathe in the smell of *borsch*, and imagine I am at home, with Baba.

One of the doors swishes open and the Old Yaga steps in, wearing heavy leather gloves and thick glass goggles on her forehead. "Are you all right, Marinka?"

I stare at her, wondering why she's wearing the gloves and goggles. "I'm fine. It's just…" My throat tightens. I don't know where to begin. A tear escapes from one of my eyes and I wipe it away with the back of my hand.

"Have you been with those two girls again, by any chance?"

I nod and sniff. "Never again. I hate the living."

"Really?" The Old Yaga peels off her gloves and lifts the kettle over the fire. "Why is that?"

"Because they hate us," I say bitterly.

"I don't think so. Those girls you've been talking to are just young and silly, perhaps a little afraid of things that are different. But not all the living are like that. I have lots of kind and thoughtful, living friends."

"You have living friends?" I sit up straighter and look at the Old Yaga, a tingle running along my spine. "But Yaga aren't allowed to be friends with the living."

"Not really, no, so I'd rather you didn't tell anyone, but I like the living. That's why I chose to settle in the market when my house retired."

I stare at her, open-mouthed. "But Baba said Yaga are supposed to protect the houses and The Gates. She said we should be wary of the living."

"And she was absolutely right." The Old Yaga pours some tea and beckons me over to the table. "I've got myself into trouble more than once by talking to the living."

"So why do you do it?"

"Same reason you do, I suspect."

I look down at my tea. The Old Yaga seems so happy with her life that I doubt she talks to the living for the same reasons as me, because she wants to escape her destiny and her loneliness and join them. But I can't tell the Old Yaga that, because I'm supposed to be convincing her that I want to be the next Guardian. "I've realized being friends with the living isn't worth it," I say firmly. "I'd rather have no friends than friends like Lamya and Salma."

"Those girls can be pretty cruel," the Old Yaga agrees. "Don't give up on the living though. There are more good people than bad people in this world. You just have to be careful, and choose your friends wisely."

"I don't need friends." The words taste sour in my mouth. "Besides, there's no point making friends with the living when the house moves on all the time anyway."

"Spoken like a true Yaga." The Old Yaga takes a swig of tea and smiles.

I shift uncomfortably in my seat. "Can we get ready for the Ceremony of Bonding now?" I ask. "You said you'd help me cook."

"That's what I was doing when you arrived." The Old Yaga's eyes light up. "Except I'm making something a bit more exciting than *borsch*. Come and see."

I follow her through the door she came out of earlier. Strange chemical smells tickle my nose and my gaze drifts along the walls in awe. Huge copper pots and pipes fill one side of the room. They are held firmly in place by shoots, roots and vines growing around them.

The other side of the room is dominated by a long wooden bench. Above it, the house has grown shelves that are packed with all kinds of glass containers, with tightly coiled tendrils wrapped around them.

"Isn't it wonderful?" The Old Yaga looks around the room proudly. "The house grew me this laboratory over eight hundred years ago, and it holds every boiling pot and test tube so carefully that nothing has ever broken in here. Not even when the house used to gallop across The Steppes." She turns to me and winks. "Or when it rolls over to entertain visitors."

"What's it all for?" I whisper, my eyes wide from trying to take everything in. The copper drums shine so bright they blind me, so I turn to the shelves and stare at all the bottles filled with powders, granules and liquids of every colour imaginable.

"This is for making spirit *trost*." The Old Yaga waves at the copper-filled side of the room, then turns to the bench and beams. "While this is for my experiments and concoctions. Right now I'm making fireworks."

"Fireworks?" Tiny explosions pop through my body and I look at the things on the bench more closely. Round balls, like paper onions, are laid out neatly, a piece of string dangling from each of them. One of the onions is open, revealing layers of black powder and paper twists inside it.

"For tonight." The Old Yaga pulls her gloves back on and grins at me. "Do you want to help?"

"Yes, please." I nod, my fingers quivering. All

thoughts of Salma and Lamya evaporate as I pull on the gloves and goggles the Old Yaga passes me and move towards the bench.

"You can make the stars." The Old Yaga taps the bottom of the shelves and a thick vine creeps down to the bench, carrying a rack full of colourful powders. "These are what give the fireworks their colour."

The Old Yaga pulls the bottles out of the rack one by one and tells me the names of the powders inside them, and what colours they burn: barium chloride burns pale green, calcium chloride orange, and sodium nitrate yellow. She also explains how I can mix up new colours; for example, by blending strontium carbonate that burns red with copper chloride that burns blue, I can make purple explosions. Then she shows me how much powder to put into each twist and leaves me to it.

I make up the little stars at one end of the bench while the Old Yaga works at the other end. I start by using one powder in each twist, but soon I'm adding a little of this and a little of that, wondering what marvellous colours might erupt into the sky later on.

The Old Yaga adds my stars to her paper onions, excitedly telling me about all the layers and what they do. She says the onions are actually called aerial shells and there is a lifting charge to take them up into the sky, a bursting charge to explode them, and a time fuse to make sure the shells explode at the right height.

"How did you learn how to do all this?" I ask when she pauses for breath.

"From the living! That's why I talk to them; to learn new things about the world, and myself. I've always had living friends, ever since I made my first friend on The Steppes when I was about your age.

He was a dark-haired nomad boy who dazzled me with magic tricks." The Old Yaga wiggles her fingers, pulls a shiny coin out of the air and smiles. "But I learned firework-making much later, from Master Jiao in the Far East. I've always loved chemistry, although back then, centuries ago, it wasn't called chemistry. I studied alchemy with monks and scholars from many different lands. We knew so little in those days, we were convinced we could make gold using egg shells and manure. You can't imagine the stink in here when we experimented." She laughs, her eyes sparkling. "Things have come a long way since then.

I've studied with some of the greatest chemists: Boyle, Lavoisier, Rosalind Franklin." She sighs. "It seems like only yesterday I was having classes with Mendeleev, but that must be over a century ago now."

"How old are you?" I ask.

"Didn't your Baba tell you it's rude to ask an Elder her age?" The Old Yaga peers at me sternly through her goggles, but she's still smiling so I think she must be joking.

"I'm sorry." I blush. "Baba told me you were an Ancient Elder, but I've never really thought about what that means. I just figured you were old and wise or something."

"Old, yes. Ancient Elders are Yaga who have lived more than one thousand years. But wisdom doesn't always come with age, although I'd like to think I've learned a few things over the years."

"Like chemistry?"

The Old Yaga nods. "You have to fill your time with more than just guiding the dead. Your Baba always liked music, didn't she?"

"She could fix and play every musical instrument

I ever saw," I say proudly, picturing Baba tapping her foot and playing her accordion, tilting her head to kiss her flute to her lips, and strumming on her *balalaika*. I blink away the welling tears and remind myself that tonight I'm going to bring her home.

"What about you?" the Old Yaga asks. "What do you like to do?"

I put down the star I've just twisted and think. My mouth tightens into a thin line, because I don't know what I like to do. There are the everyday things, of course, like reading and daydreaming, but I don't have a passion. Not like Benjamin with his art, or Nina with her plants and animals, the Old Yaga with her chemistry, or Baba with her music. Sparks flash in my mind as I realize that is what I want to do: I want to explore the world, and try new things, and find out what my passion is. But to do that I need to bring Baba home, so she can be Guardian. Instead of me.

"I just want to be a Guardian," I lie, thinking about the ceremony tonight and finding Baba.

The Old Yaga pulls off her gloves and goggles and admires the neat stack of shells in front of us.

"That should be enough, I think."

I slide up my goggles and, glancing out of the window, notice it's nearly dark outside already. "Is it time to go?" I ask, my stomach tightening.

"If you're sure you still want to do this." The Old Yaga lifts a big metal box from under the bench and starts packing the shells into it.

"Of course. I can't wait." I smile, realizing it's true. Tonight I'm going to see more Yaga in one place than I've ever seen. I'm going to watch the fireworks I made explode above me, and I'm going through The Gate to bring my grandmother home.

Tonight is going to be wonderful. And tomorrow, Baba will be home to guide the dead, the crack in the house will heal, the great cycle will be back in balance, and I will be free to figure out what I want to do with my life.

Perhaps then being dead, stuck in a house with chicken legs, might not be so bad after all.

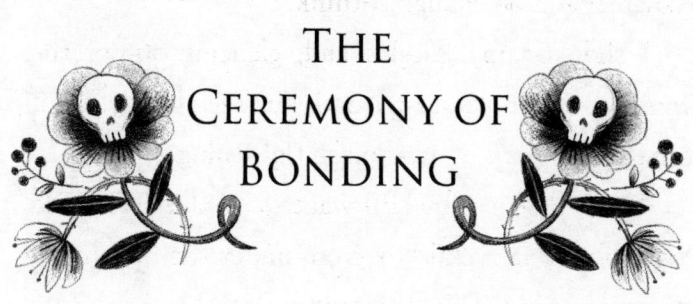

THE CEREMONY OF BONDING

The Old Yaga leans out of the window and whoops with delight. "I'd forgotten what it was like to be in a house running so fast." She pulls her head back inside the house and beams, her thick coily hair all puffed up from the wind. Fresh vines fall from the rafters, thickening and twisting into a hammock beneath her. "Why thank you, my lady."

"Lady?" I raise an eyebrow.

"Of course." The Old Yaga hops into the set. "Your house is a fine lady."

"How do you know?" I ask. I've never thought of my house as being a "he" or a "she".

"Just a feeling. Look!" Her arm flies up and points at something on the horizon. A small blur, barely visible in the moonlight, is growing larger by the second. Jack paces across the window sill as he stares at it.

I move closer and squint at the blur. "It's another house!"

"It's Yaga Onekin! I haven't seen him in…goodness it must be two hundred years at least." The Old Yaga moves her hand over her heart and smiles.

The other house draws closer, until it is galloping right alongside us. My heart thumps faster as the pounding of two sets of enormous chicken feet now reverberates through my body.

An old man in a bright yellow bowler hat waves from the window. "Greetings, Yaga Tatyana!" he shouts. "You look even more beautiful than I remember."

The Old Yaga giggles and waves her handkerchief at him. "Why thank you, Yaga Onekin. You are looking good yourself. It's a fine night for a party."

"It certainly is." Yaga Onekin looks up at the moon. It's big, bright and full. "I'll race you there." His house pulls in front of us, sending a cloud of dust whirling through the window. Jack squawks loudly and flaps up onto my shoulder.

"Are you going to stand for that, House?" The Old Yaga grips the hammock vines and our house accelerates hard. I stumble, and have to lean on the window sill to stop from falling over. The house is running faster than ever before, the landscape whizzing past in a blur. Excitement explodes through my body and I scream into the rushing air.

"Faster! Go on, House! You can do it! Faster! Faster!"

Jack mimics my shouts, lifting his beak high and flapping his wings.

The house's feet drum, harder and faster, and soon we're level with Yaga Onekin's house again. He smiles and tips his hat as we overtake him, and the Old Yaga nods her head in return. I cheer and jump into the air. "I knew you could do it, House!" I slap the window sill in triumph.

The Old Yaga laughs and swings back in her hammock.

"Is that your name?" I ask. "Tatyana?"

"Yes, Yaga Marinka." The Old Yaga nods and holds out her hand. "I'm Yaga Tatyana. Very pleased to meet you."

I give her hand a squeeze, and then blush. I can't believe I've never even thought to ask her name before. "Will you know all the Yaga there tonight?" I ask.

"Yes. They all visit the market to buy my spirit *trost*. That's the reason I make it." She winks. "I like making friends, even if they do move on."

More Yaga houses appear on the horizon and join us, dust trails flying out behind them. The air thrums with the sound of so many chicken feet, and I tremble with the thrill of it all.

"I've never seen so many houses!" I exclaim.

"A thunder of Yaga houses is a wonderful sight." The Old Yaga sighs. "It doesn't happen enough."

"Why don't Yaga get together more often?" I ask, although I think I know the answer already.

"It is our duty to protect the houses and The Gates from the living. Gatherings this size might draw unwanted attention." The Old Yaga waves her words away as if they are a bad smell and looks at me out of the corners of her eyes. "I've always thought it would be nice if we did meet more though. Being Yaga can be lonely."

"Not really," I lie, not wanting her to think I'm not ready for the ceremony. "Every night we get to party with the dead."

"True." The Old Yaga nods. "I've always loved the guiding parties. Wait until you see a Yaga party though. There is nothing quite like it. Talking of which, I'm going to get ready." She jumps down from the hammock and opens the big case she brought with her. Clothes burst out of it. She rummages past a huge puffy dress and a tiny one that looks like it's made from nothing but tassels. "I'm afraid I've never been very good at packing." A furry hat, frilly collar and feather boa get thrown to one side, along with a small bag decorated with fragments of abalone shell that shimmer with the colours of the ocean.

"I thought you might want to borrow something, but I wasn't sure what you'd like." The Old Yaga holds up a squashed blue hairpiece that might have been shaped like a boat once and laughs. "I suppose these went out of fashion a while ago. I really should have a clear-out."

"I'm happy in this." I smooth my plain woollen

dress down, although I can't stop my gaze from wandering to her case.

"Whatever you're comfortable in." The Old Yaga wanders off with a long black skirt and white top embroidered with flowers. "But feel free to have a look while I get changed."

There are so many interesting fabrics and designs poking out of her case that I find myself flicking through them, trying to work out where and when they are from. Near the bottom of the pile I find a black velvet dress with colourful skulls and flowers all round the edges. It feels warm and soft, and thick enough that Jack's claws shouldn't damage it, and the pattern reminds me of Baba.

"That looks lovely on you." The Old Yaga smiles when she emerges to find me wearing it. "Tonight will be so much fun." She hops back into her hammock and looks out of the window. "Whether you go ahead with the bonding or not."

"What do you mean? Of course I'm going ahead with the bonding," I say firmly.

"I'm just saying, if you change your mind, that's

fine. It's a big decision, bonding, especially for someone like you—"

"Someone dead, you mean?" I interrupt, a cold feeling trickling down my neck.

"No. Someone so young," the Old Yaga says gently.

Blood rises into my cheeks. "Sorry," I mumble, embarrassed about speaking so sharply. I turn back to the window and think about the night ahead; the ceremony, going through The Gate, and drifting to the stars. Because I'm dead, I'll float over the black ocean and the glassy mountains. Then I'll find Baba and carry her home, the way she carried me home as a baby. "I'm absolutely sure I want to do this," I say. "I'm not going to change my mind."

The noise of the chicken feet becomes deeper, more echoing. "The Steppes," the Old Yaga whispers, gazing out of the window with sparkling eyes. "It's wonderful to be back. I've always thought of this as my home."

Grassland, shining silver in the moonlight, stretches as far as I can see. The chicken feet thump over the earth and the scent of fresh rain rises up from the ground. In the distance are the dark outlines of low mountains and the even blacker silhouette of a forest.

The house slows to a canter, rolling towards the treeline, and the other Yaga houses do the same. As we draw closer I hear drums on the breeze. The drumming seems to lift me up, so I feel lighter and taller. Jack flaps back to the window sill, his eyes shining as he looks eagerly out into the night.

My whole body tingles when I see the gathering at the edge of the forest. I've never imagined anything like it. A huge skeleton fence glows orange with the light of a thousand skulls. Beyond it, scores of Yaga houses are jumping and dancing to music that flows from their open doors. A few older houses are sat, legs folded beneath them, at the edge of the group, watching some younger houses play with a stitched leather ball as big as a cow.

Bones tumble from my skeleton store and run to join the others in the fence. Femurs and fibulas assemble into a strange cart that rattles along the top of the fence precariously. "You should go for a ride, have some fun." The Old Yaga ushers me out of the door. "Oh, wait a moment, I have something of yours. You dropped it outside my stall a few nights ago." She pulls Baba's headscarf, the one with the skulls and flowers, out of her pocket and ties it under my chin. "There." She walks down the porch steps with me and points at a puddle on the damp earth. "What do you see now?"

I peer into the water and see my hair curling out from under Baba's scarf. "My reflection!" I lean closer. "I look like a Guardian!"

"Almost." The Old Yaga chuckles. "I'll see you at the ceremony."

I walk towards the crowd, fizzing with nerves, and before I know what's happening I'm surrounded by Ancient Elders, shaking my hands and patting me on the back.

"I'm Yaga Ana…"

"…Yaga Dmitry…"

"…delighted to meet you…"

"…wonderful night for a bonding…"

"…what a splendid house…"

"Yaga Elena! Come and meet Yaga Marinka."

A young girl runs up and my smile widens. I've never seen a Yaga as young as me before.

"Hello, Yaga Marinka. Congratulations on your bonding." Yaga Elena smiles back, like she's known me all her life, links her arm through mine and leads me away from the Elders. "Shall we go on the bone coaster?"

I follow Yaga Elena's gaze to the top of the fence, where there are now several bone carts rattling along. Yaga Elena leads me to a spot where the fence is low and one of the carts drops down to us with a clatter. We clamber inside, sit on pelvic bone seats and lean back against shoulder blades. Then my stomach lurches as the cart whooshes up to the top of the fence, where a skeleton track rises and falls in a great circle around all the Yaga Houses.

Jack soars above us as we hurtle along, clutching each other tight on the rickety ascents and screaming together on the frantic descents. Everything is bright lights and swirls, dizziness and laughter and stars in my eyes. When the cart finally stops, I stumble out with wobbly legs and a huge smile on my face.

Yaga are everywhere, laying food on long tables and talking so fast it makes my head spin. They are all really friendly. They smile and compliment me and my house, and feed Jack scraps of food with their fingers. Some of them tell me how they knew my Baba, and how lovely she was. I smile back at them, holding in my secret. That Baba is not gone; that I am going to rescue her soon.

I meet so many of the Yaga, but get to know none. They dance and drift away, like the dead at a guiding, but my cheeks ache from smiling because they are Yaga, like me. Well, almost like me. I don't fit in with the living and I don't fit in with the dead, but here I feel like maybe I could, if there was enough time. It's such a shame it won't last. The Old Yaga was right; Yaga should get together more often. When Baba returns, I wonder if we can somehow arrange another gathering.

"Look!" Yaga Elena tugs on my arm. "They've decorated your house."

I turn to see my house illuminated by strings of skull candles dangling from the roof, and covered with chains of huge red flowers. It looks so beautiful I swell with pride.

"Are you excited about your bonding?" Yaga Elena asks.

I nod, my nerves charging with electricity. "Have you bonded with your house?" I ask.

"Oh, no," Yaga Elena replies. "I live with my mother, Yaga Valentyna. I don't want to be a Guardian until I'm at least fifty. Maybe one hundred. I think you're very brave doing this so young."

I don't feel brave. All of a sudden I feel very cold and unsure of myself. The thought of leaving all these Yaga, and the light and music of the ceremony, to step alone into the darkness of The Gate makes me shiver.

The Old Yaga appears at my side, carrying several thick metal tubes. Yaga Onekin is with her, holding the metal box I know is filled with the fireworks we made earlier. "Do you want to light the first shells?" she asks with a smile.

"Yes, please," I say. "But what about Benji and Jack? Will they get scared?"

"Who is Benji?" Yaga Elena asks.

"My lamb. He's in a shelter on the back porch."

"I'll stay with him and Jack while you light the fireworks if you like," Yaga Elena offers.

"That would be kind. Thank you." I show Elena to where Benji is tucked up in his blankets, and give both Benji and Jack a stroke and a squeeze before I leave them. Tears prick the back of my eyes but I blink them away, telling myself that going through The Gate will be worth it. I'll return soon, with Baba.

Hundreds of Yaga are gathered on and around the front porch of my house, their faces shining in the light of the skulls. The Old Yaga leads me a short distance away from them, and shows me how to set up the tubes, which she calls mortars, for firing the firework shells.

Yaga Onekin helps me to light the first five and we run back to the porch and watch as enormous red, green, gold, blue and purple dandelions burst into the sky. Cheers rise up from the crowd and as the last glittering sparks float down to the ground, I'm swept into the familiar smells and warmth of my house.

Five Ancient Elders gather around the space where The Gate always opens, and sing something loud and joyful in the language of the dead. Yaga stream into the room until it is bursting with life. They clap, stamp their feet and dance, and pass around plates of food and glasses of *kvass*. The house bounces to the beat and the hearth smiles up at me with a look of satisfaction.

A necklace of tiny white flowers falls around my neck and I look up to see thin vines, laden with blossoms, all over the house. They are growing from the rafters, swaying in the air above, creeping down the walls, and draping the mantelpiece and furniture. The Yagas nudge me towards The Gate and as I move forwards the vines and flowers curl gently around me, linking me to the house. I feel the house's happiness like warmth inside me.

"Remember you don't have to do this, Marinka. It's fine to change your mind," the Old Yaga whispers into my ear.

I move away from her, and let the sweet scent of the flowers envelop me. Silky petals and soft fuzzy vines brush over my hands and face as I draw closer to The Gate. When I am right next to the Ancient Elders, they turn to me and change their song. It becomes slow and solemn. I try to make out the words but I can't focus. My heart is pounding in my chest.

The song quietens until it is barely more than a whisper. I think it's something about the beauty of the great cycle and the honour of being a Guardian. I sweep the vines from my hands and try to slow my breathing.

Yaga gather around me, still and calm, their lips parted in anticipation. A draught flows down the chimney and the candles flicker, sending shadows dancing around the room.

"Yaga House!" one of the Ancient Elders shouts up to the rafters so loud I flinch. "Open The Gate so Yaga Marinka can make her promise to you with the stars as her witness."

This is it. The Gate is going to open, just a few steps away, and I'm finally going to bring Baba home.

I'll be safe again, and the house will stop crumbling. The unguided dead will stop fading away and the great cycle will swing back into balance. All the worries that have been crushing me since Baba left will drift away as I pull her close, and she will hold me tight and make everything all right. The house will heal, she'll guide the dead, and I will take control of my future.

A long deep breath swells my chest. And the moment the black rectangle of The Gate appears, I run towards it, as fast as I can, and jump.

DARKNESS

Everything slows as I fly towards The Gate. Flowered vines break and fall around me. The jaws of the Yaga drop open and they breathe in sharply. Some place hands over their mouths. Eyes widen in shock and lights, reflected from deep inside the void, flicker across their pupils. Air rushes past my ears and the tide of the black ocean pulls me downwards. I brace myself as cold currents reach up and creep over my head and neck...

But then claws dig into my back, someone grabs my arm, and a fierce pain tears through my head as it connects with the floor. Darkness and silence engulf me, punctuated by the faint sound of a *balalaika* playing my favourite lullaby.

My eyelids flicker open and I see a collection of blurry Yaga faces leaning over me with crinkled, concerned expressions. I squeeze my eyes shut again and a hot angry tear burns its way down to my ear. I wish I could sink into the floorboards and disappear.

Yaga voices murmur above me. "Is she all right?"

"What was she doing?"

"I think she tried to jump into The Gate."

"Why would she do that?"

"How strange."

"Is the party over?"

If only I could make my ears shut like my eyes. I don't want to see them or hear them. My head is pulsing where I banged it on the floor, my back sore where Jack scratched me, and my arm aching from being yanked. But worse than all of that is the blistering, withering feeling caused by all the Yaga staring down at me, talking about me.

"Is she conscious?"

"Should we move her?"

"Marinka?"

"Are you all right?"

"She's fine." I hear the Old Yaga's voice right next to me and feel her hand on my head.

"Let's give them some space." Yaga Onekin's voice rises above the rest, and I feel a rush of gratitude towards him as he clears the room.

My lungs ache, and I realize I've been holding my breath. Rolling onto my side, away from the Old Yaga, I peep up at The Gate. It's gone. I knew it would be, but that doesn't stop the tears from falling. They drip onto the floor as anger rushes up my neck. "Why?" I cry, my voice all gurgly, then I crumple into a ball as pain explodes through my head.

"Can you carry Marinka to her bedroom?" the Old Yaga asks, squashing something cold against my forehead. "You've had a nasty bump, Marinka, but you'll be fine. Just try to rest for a moment."

Yaga Onekin's yellow bowler hat dips over me, his arms slide under me, and I'm lifted into the air. Dark spots cloud my vision and my body is swallowed by a heavy numbness.

The Old Yaga and Yaga Onekin whisper by my door, and then there is silence.

Jack lands on my headboard and pushes his beak into my ear. I close my eyes and turn away from him, my head throbbing. I was so close. I could have got Baba back. If only…

I drift in and out of an uncomfortable sleep. The house rolls rhythmically, its chicken feet drumming beneath me. I try to tell it to stop but my voice doesn't work. I try to move but the sheets feel like ropes, the bed like a cage.

Finally the house slows and lurches to the ground. It keeps on tilting and I slide down the bed. I reach for the headboard, too late. My body thumps onto the floor and the floorboards push and roll me towards the front door.

"What's going on?" I croak, trying to scramble to my feet. The front door opens, I skid through and am bumped down each of the porch steps until I land in a heap on the hard dry earth outside the house. I sit up, blink and rub my neck. We're back in the market.

It's dark, and the world is spinning.

The Old Yaga walks calmly down the steps after me. Behind her the door swings shut and all the windows slide closed.

"What's going on?" I ask again. "House? What are you doing?"

The house rises up and turns its back to me.

"Your house is upset with you." The Old Yaga helps me to my feet.

"Why?" My voice sounds whiny. I clear my throat and try again. "Why are you upset?" This time I sound angry. I kick the rear porch in frustration and the house shuffles away from me.

"Come on." The Old Yaga squeezes my arm. "Your house is tired. She's run a long way tonight. Let her rest. You can make up in the morning."

I let the Old Yaga lead me away from my house, along the dark empty streets of the market, and past the skulls and bottles of her spirit *trost* stall. The lintel above the Old Yaga's front door welcomes us with a smile. The front room is warm, smelling of fireworks and *borsch*. I flop into a chair by the fire, my head aching and foggy. "Why is my house so upset with me?" I ask the Old Yaga as she passes me a mug of cocoa. "I don't understand."

"No one likes to be tricked." The Old Yaga sits opposite me. "Your house thought you were going to bond with her tonight, but you just wanted to go through The Gate."

"I was going to bring Baba home." Anger burns my eyes and my voice rises, "Why didn't the house understand that? Why didn't Jack understand that? Why don't you understand that? Why did you all have to interfere? I could have got Baba back if you hadn't stopped me." I glare at the Old Yaga, my breath coming in short jagged gasps that hurt my lungs.

"We stopped you because we care. Going through The Gate is dangerous. You might never return."

"It's worth the risk!" I yell. "I'd do anything to bring Baba home. And it's my decision anyway – you had no right!"

"Your Baba is gone," the Old Yaga says quietly.

"You're wrong!" I shout, rising to my feet. My head spins, and my mug falls and smashes on the floor.

I stare down at my hands, and see the broken mug and spilled cocoa right through them. My whole body fades and for a moment I feel light and fleeting as morning mist. Then I flicker back and breath rushes into my lungs.

"Sit down, Marinka, please." The Old Yaga reaches for my hand but I pull away from her and stagger to the door. Pushing it open, I pick up speed and burst out into the market.

It's cold and dark, but it's that hazy darkness, just before dawn. A few market traders are setting up their stalls, rubbing their hands together and breathing little white clouds into the air. I race past them.

I need my house. And I need Baba. The Old Yaga is wrong; I can bring Baba home, and I will. Baba will make everything all right.

My vision blurs. I stop to wait for the world to swing back into focus and the familiar, comforting scent of woodsmoke wraps around me. I breathe in deeply, straighten my spine and walk calmly on, back towards my house.

The smell of woodsmoke grows stronger. It curls

through the air, thickening as I draw closer to home.
I walk faster, break into a run again. Something is
wrong. The smoke is too thick.

Cracks of burning, splitting wood break the silence.
A jackdaw shrieks. I sprint as fast I can, lungs heaving,
legs pounding the ground. I hear people shouting and
the splash of water. I round the corner and see it.
What I was trying not to think. The house, my house,
is on fire.

FIRE

"We didn't mean to set it on fire." Salma runs in front of me, arms outstretched as if she can block my view of the house. Tears are streaming down her face, leaving thick trails in the soot and ash coating her skin. "We were going to help my father set up his stall but we noticed your house was facing the other way and we thought that was strange so we were just looking and then Lamya thought she saw giant legs under your porch and bones on the floor and I said that was stupid so I lit the match to prove her wrong and" – she takes a deep, juddering breath – "I saw a skull and I panicked and fell and then there was fire everywhere and we couldn't put it out. It all happened so quickly. I'm so, so sorry." Her face crumples in confusion. "Why is there a skull under your house?"

I push past Salma and run to my house, but strong arms grip my shoulders and a deep voice tells me it's not safe. Men and women rush back and forth, carrying water and shouting to each other. Lamya is sitting on the floor, rocking and muttering something about skulls and huge claws.

This is all my fault. If I hadn't kept Nina from The Gate, Baba wouldn't have gone with her, and I wouldn't have ended up here in this stupid market with Lamya and Salma. Why couldn't they leave my house alone?

Smoke billows into the night sky. My whole house is burning, blackening inside a monstrous, roaring fire. Like the fire that took away my parents, and my life. I stare at it in disbelief. For as long as I can remember I've been haunted by visions of a Yaga house in flames. But this is real, right in front of me, a fire blazing hotter and huger than I ever could have imagined. Threatening to take away everything I love now: my house, Jack, Benji. All my hopes for the future.

"Jack!" I shout, struggling against the arms holding me. The walls of the house creak and crackle and my body flickers. Like the wispy dead, I pass right through the arms holding me and rush towards the house.

"Jack!" I call again, as loud as I can, then cough as ash-filled air hits the back of my throat. He flies down out of the smoke, smashes into my shoulder and scrambles into my arms. "Jack," I sob. "Where's Benji?"

Jack flaps awkwardly towards the back of the house, and I race after him. The porch is alive with flames. I lift my arms to shield my face from the intense heat and edge closer to the fire. Benji is bleating madly, banging against the bones of his shelter.

I step onto the porch, the heat and smoke burning my lungs. My dress feels like it is melting onto my skin. Benji pushes his head through the gap near the water butt and calls me urgently. I kick the water butt once, twice, three times and it crashes over, splashing the bones and sending steam into the air. The flames fall back a little and I fumble with the latch on the shelter, but my fingers keep fading in and out.

Before I can open the shelter, the whole house lurches sideways and I have to grab the balustrade to stay upright. The ground swings away as the house rises up, its legs on fire, crackling in the heat. People shout and scream below, their shocked faces shining through the smoke.

"Stop!" I yell, squeezing the balustrade with both hands. "The living can see!" But then I realize there's no choice. Putting the fire out is far more important.

The house runs, faster and faster, jumping over people, market stalls, and buildings. Flames and smoke fly behind us like hair. Burned shards of wood fall to the ground like tiny meteors in slow motion, and sparks dance like fireflies around us. The blur of harbour lights reflected in the calm of the ocean lies ahead.

With a final giant leap, the house soars through the air and lands with a sizzling splash in the water. A cold wave slaps over me. Benji cries and Jack squawks loudly. I slip on the floorboards and taste salt and charcoal on my lips.

The house creaks and sighs, sloshing from side to side until all the flames are extinguished and we're

273

sitting in a great smouldering cloud of acrid smoke. Jack flaps onto my lap amid a spray of gritty water. I wrap my arm around him, drag us both to the back door and push it open. He slops into the house, a mass of slippery wet feathers, and I go back for Benji.

By the time we're all safe inside the damp, blackened front room, the house is on the move again. Splashing through the shallows, stepping over sand, running through the desert and climbing uphill, into mountains and forest.

I find blankets on the high shelves in Baba's room. They stink of smoke, but at least they're dry. I peel off my clothes and wrap myself in them, sit in Baba's chair with Benji on my lap and Jack on my shoulder, and we sway gently together as the house gallops on through the night.

"I'm so sorry," I whisper to the rafters. "I didn't mean to trick you, or upset you. It's just that I miss Baba so much. Bringing her home means everything to me. She is the only person I have ever known and loved, and I'm scared to live without her. I need her. Not just so she can guide the dead and save me from being Guardian. I need her here, to love me and keep me safe."

A vine curls down from the rafters and wraps around me. It thickens as it holds me close, and I lean my head against its soft, velvety bark. Tendrils coil over Baba's headscarf, which is bunched up in my hands, and as they entwine with the fabric I realize for the first time that the house misses Baba too.

"Take us somewhere deserted," I say. "Somewhere with no people at all." I've had enough of the living. I want things to go back to the way they were. Just me, Baba and the house, guiding the dead.

THE LAND OF SNOW

My teeth chattering wakes me. Cold air rattles into my lungs. My eyes are frozen shut and won't open until I warm them with my hands, and then they feel scratchy and sore. Tears well as I look around the room. Everything is black with soot, grey with ash, or white with ice and snow. There are holes in the roof, walls and floor. So much of the house has been reduced to crumbling charcoal, I can't imagine how long it will take to grow back. A sick feeling swells in my stomach.

I rise to my feet, my limbs heavy and slow, and pick my way across the floor to the window. Floorboards disintegrate beneath my steps and I wince. Benji follows me, shivering as he skids over icy patches, so I

pick him up and tuck him back in the blankets wrapped around me.

The light through the window is soft and subdued. It's impossible to tell what time of day it is. The sun is hidden behind a thick white sky and endless snow stretches out, smooth and flat in every direction. The landscape is empty, devoid of life. This is what I asked for, but now that I'm faced with it my body seems to rebel. The urge to run somewhere, anywhere, is overwhelming, but there is nowhere to go.

Jack jumps off my shoulder, lands on the window sill and taps on the glass. The sash judders slowly up as flecks of blackened wood rain down. Icy air rolls into the room and nips at my skin. I pull my blankets tighter around my chest and Jack ruffles up his feathers. Then he half lifts his wings, like he can't decide whether to go out for a fly or not.

"There's nothing out there, Jack. Come on, let's build a fire."

The house flinches at the word and my heart plummets through my chest. I don't want to look at a flame ever again either, but it's the only way to dry

the house and we'll all freeze without one.

All the wood in the store is soaked through. I eye up the furniture, but that's wet too. I stare up at the rafters, wondering what to burn, and one of them cracks loudly and falls to the floor with a bang.

"Thank you, House." I smile. The gesture feels like a hug. "We'll get you fixed up in no time," I say, hoping it's true.

I fetch the axe and split the rafter into logs and kindling. It's hard work but it warms me, and the feeling I'm doing something useful cheers me up a little.

Once the fire is roaring I pile almost everything in the house around the hearth to dry out. Thankfully most of the food is fine, kept safe inside tins and jars with tightly sealed lids. I feed Benji, and make a huge bowl of hot *kasha* with damson jelly for me and Jack, then start to clean the house.

Soot, ash and charcoal are everywhere. I melt cauldrons of snow over the fire and scrub everything from roof to floor. Then I do it again because it's still grey and gritty. By the time I'm finished, my back and arms ache, and my fingers are red and sore. And the house still looks dirty. I flop into Baba's chair and put my head in my hands.

Silence and emptiness surround me. Talking to Jack or Benji or the house doesn't help. My voice echoing through the quiet, still air just highlights the fact I'm alone. As the day draws on, I feel overwhelmed by the mess, the damage and the loneliness.

Everything reminds me of Baba, from the blackened cooking pots to the charred musical instruments in the corner, to the tasks I'm trying to do, because I know Baba would do them ten times better and ten times faster than me.

I wish she was here to help, and to talk to. But more than anything I just wish I could sit with her one more time, apologize for all the stupid things I ever said and did, and tell her that I love her.

The Old Yaga drifts through my thoughts too. At first thinking of her makes me hot with anger, because she stopped me going through The Gate to bring Baba home. But after a while I realize I miss her too. It was fun rolling in her house, and building fireworks, and racing Yaga Onekin on the way to the ceremony. I wonder how she's doing, back in the market, and whether my house running in plain sight caused any trouble for her. But then I picture her standing tall, proud and confident, and I realize if anyone can quash rumours about a house running it will be her.

Thinking about what she and the other Yaga must think of me makes my skin prickle though. To them I am just a foolish child. They don't understand how much I need Baba.

Behind the grubby windows the sky fades into a thick, grey dusk. I light some candles and carry on cleaning. Even when night falls I don't go to bed because I'm afraid the fire might burn up, out of control, or burn out and we'll all freeze in our sleep. I end up dozing on Baba's chair, waking up every time the scrubbing brush falls from my hand.

By the morning I'm more exhausted than I've ever been, but looking around the house I feel a swell of pride. It looks almost clean, and already there are signs of the house healing.

New wood is growing over the scorched sections

of the window frames and walls. Thick mats of moss and grass have covered the holes in the floor, and vines have tangled their way across the gaps in the roof. A fat shoot is even extending from the place the rafter fell from. I bounce out into the cold, eager to check the outside of the house.

The porch balustrades are coiling into new patterns, and the chicken legs are thickening. I breathe a sigh of relief. But then I see the crumbling crack near the skeleton store.

Dead wood surrounds the open rift, spreading up to the roof and all the way to the far corner of the house. The wall is charred and black, crusted over with soot-filled ice. At least a quarter of the front of the house is showing no sign of healing at all. With no one guiding the dead, the house can't heal completely.

"House." I sit on the porch steps and wrap my arms around my fluttering belly. "We need Baba to guide the dead. Or you are going to wither away."

The house shakes from side to side.

"But I can't guide the dead on my own." My eyes fill with tears.

The balustrade curves down and tries to pull back my crumpling shoulders.

"No." I shake my head, wriggling my shoulders away from the wood. "I'm not strong enough on my own. I need Baba."

Spindles poke into my back as they try to straighten my spine.

"Stop it." I shuffle along the step. "I can bring Baba home to guide. I know I can, if only you'll let me through The Gate."

All the windows slide shut and the house burrows down into the snow.

I turn and stare at the endless white, every muscle in my body cramped tight. Silence presses against my ears, occasionally broken by the sound of the crack widening or a shard of wood splitting and falling into the snow.

At first the noises of the house crumbling make me hot with anger, because it feels like the house is trying to force me into guiding. But that isn't true.

The house closed The Gate to stop me going through it. The Old Yaga said it was dangerous to go through, and I might never return. So the house was trying to protect me, even though by doing so it has ended up hurting itself.

My heart sinks. I don't want to guide. But I can't let the house continue suffering. Not when I could do something to save it.

"Fine," I say finally. "I'll guide the dead and I won't try to go through The Gate."

The house peeps a window open and peers at me suspiciously.

"It's not a trick, and I'm not lying." I take a long, deep breath. "I can't watch you crumble and splinter and fall apart. I can't lose you too. Not because losing you might mean I fade away," I add. "It's because you're my family. And I love you."

The house smiles, with its windows and door and the eaves of the porch roof, but there is something sad about it too. The smile is not as big and bright as it should be. I shake my head as I rise to my feet. Sometimes it's difficult to figure out what my house with chicken legs is thinking.

"Come on then," I say, blinking back tears I don't

understand. "Open the skeleton store and I'll build the fence."

I clean the bones and push them through the icy crust. As they sink into the snow my hopes and dreams for the future sink into a hidden chamber of my heart, a place so deep inside me I'm worried I'll never find them again.

Swallowing back the lump in my throat, I tell myself this is only for a night or two. I'll guide some dead and the house will heal. Perhaps then I'll be able to convince the house to let me find Baba. But I feel defeated, and the thought of guiding weighs me down. I wish there was another way to help the house and make things right.

Jack and Benji root through the snow, in a fruitless search for bugs and grass, as I string vertebrate between femurs, and balance skulls on top. When the fence is complete, I gather a bucket of snow to melt into water, and go inside. I make breakfast and sift through the remaining supplies, deciding what to prepare for the guiding feast tonight.

I spend the day cooking: *borsch* from tinned vegetables, dumplings stuffed with *tushonka*, *pirog* made with dried mushrooms, and *vatrushka* using a jar of Baba's cheese sauce. I bake black bread and honey bread, prepare *zakusi* and tinned fruit *pastilas*, and chill jellied *kissel* in the snow.

The house smells of fresh bread and spices. It's warm and inviting, a fire roaring in the hearth, and I feel closer to Baba than I have since she left. I can picture her right next to me, preparing for a guiding, and it feels as if tonight, when The Gate opens, she will be just the other side.

I light the candles in the skulls at dusk, open the bone-gate, pour *kvass* into glasses and sit nervously, waiting for the dead to arrive. Ice shifts in the distance, causing a deep rumble like thunder, and the dead appear on the horizon like mist.

My stomach twists into a tight knot as I tie Baba's headscarf under my chin and open the front door to greet them. A freezing draught sweeps into the room and the fire burns brighter. The cold air, the warm fire and the sight of the dead drifting over the snow makes me feel dizzy and sick. The thought of guiding them all, by myself, is suddenly terrifying. I know I guided the old couple, and Serina and Nina, but this is different. There are so many of them. The prospect of having all their lives add to mine – thousands upon thousands of other people's memories and emotions inside my head – makes every muscle in my body tremble… My heart races and my legs seem to melt into the floorboards.

I step outside to take a breath of cold air, and I look at the crumbling wood of the front wall and remind myself why I am doing this. Then I blink away the tears in my eyes and stand tall. Ready to guide the dead.

A gust of wind rushes down the chimney, through the house and out of the front door. It swirls around the skulls, blowing every one of the candles out. I run down the porch steps to relight them. But the house rises up, grabs me with one of its big chicken feet, and throws me onto its roof, just like it used to do when I was little.

"What are you doing?" I yell as I land on a soft snowy mound next to the chimney pot. "We have to guide the dead!"

A shoot rises next to me and wipes an escaped, frozen tear from below my eye.

"I'm fine." I bat the shoot away and look at the wispy dead retreating into the darkness. "Come on, we need to guide."

Vines unfurl from under the chimney pot and wrap around me.

"I don't understand." My brow furrows. "You and Baba have always wanted me to be the next Guardian. But now I'm finally trying to take care of you, and guide the dead, you've stopped me."

Tiny blue flowers rise between my fingers, like they did when I asked the house to take me to the market. This time I think I know what they mean.

"You want me to tell you how I feel," I whisper, "honestly."

The house nods.

I pull Baba's skulls and flowers headscarf from my head and sigh. "I don't want to be a Guardian of

The Gate." My voice is tiny, wavering. I clear my throat and try to speak more firmly. "I don't want to spend my life guiding the dead, and feeling all their joys and sorrows. I want to live my own life, with my *own* joys and sorrows."

The house is still and quiet, so I go on talking, my words making me feel weaker and stronger at the same time. "I don't want the dead's lives to add to mine. I just want one life. My life. And I want to be able to choose what to do with it." I look up at the boundless sky, and all the stars shining through the darkness. "I know I'm dead, and trapped here, but I want a different destiny. And I feel, deep inside, that it must be possible."

Vines hold me tight as the house tilts, further and further, until we are both lying on our backs gazing up at the endless stars. Swirls of green Northern Lights dance across their beauty and warmth floods through me, because I think the house might finally understand.

In this universe full of possibilities there has to be another way of making things right, without being forced to accept a fate I don't want.

I rest my hand on the vines holding me and I whisper into the night, with all the stars as my witness, "I want my own life, with the chance to choose my own destiny."

Jack struts out of the front window, nuzzles into my neck and pushes a piece of *pirog* into my ear. I move my hand to wipe it away and Baba's scarf falls across my face.

"And I want Baba," I add. "I know I could bring her home, if only you'd let me try."

The house sighs and holds me closer. It rocks me to sleep under the stars, like it used to do when I was little, and in the middle of the night I feel its vines lift me up and carry me indoors and tuck me into bed.

And although I don't know what will happen next, I feel better for telling the truth, and for knowing that me and the house will figure it out together.

THE LAND
OF LAKES

I dream of the house galloping across The Steppes, the floor rolling beneath me. As soon as I wake I know we're somewhere new. The air isn't biting my throat and my eyelashes aren't frosty.

My bedroom window is open, Jack sitting on the sill. The blur of green and blue behind him is so familiar I rush to the window, my heart almost exploding out of my chest.

"The Land of Lakes!" I exclaim. We're back in the exact same spot on the rocky ledge where I met Benjamin, and adopted Benji. "Thank you, House!"

I get dressed quickly and carry Benji outside. He struggles to escape from my arms and as soon as his feet hit the ground he starts bouncing and twisting in the air. After a few minutes of running and jumping and bleating with excitement, he kneels down near a large boulder and nibbles the new shoots of grass at the base of it.

The mountains aren't as barren as I remember them. Spring has brought fresh grass and wild flowers, and the heather bushes are a rich, dark green, a few of them speckled with tiny purple buds. Jack squawks loudly as he hops and flaps over to his heather bush and flings bits of weathered rock up into the air, looking for bugs.

I gaze at the valley below, the little town by the lake and the tiny villages scattered around it, and sadness washes over me. Last time I was here I believed I could visit the town if only I could escape the house. But now I know I can never escape the house. I turn back to the front door. "Oh, House. Why did you bring me here?"

The house twists so its windows are facing Benji. He's walking slowly towards Jack, head down, grazing.

"We came here to bring Benji home?" I crumple

onto the porch steps and sigh. I know he will be better off here, where there is plenty of grass and space to roam, but he and Jack are all I have left.

Bones tumble from the skeleton store and I spin around, confused. Then something about the way the house looks at me, with its eaves slumped in resignation, makes bubbles of excitement rise through my body. "You're going to let me go through The Gate, aren't you?" I whisper the question, hardly daring to believe it.

The house nods slowly.

"Thank you!" I jump up and cover my mouth with my hands. Tears of relief and happiness roll down my cheeks and I wipe them away, laughing. "Jack!" I call, bursting to share the news with someone. He walks towards me, glancing back over his shoulder to the insect-filled rubble beneath his heather bush. "I'm going to bring Baba home!" I shout. "Tonight!"

"Who's Baba?"

I start at the voice, lift my hand over my eyes and peer in the direction it came from. Benjamin waves from the boulder we sat on together last time

I was here. "Your house walked back then?" He smiles, a familiar glint of mischief in his eyes.

"Yes. It did." A smile warms my cheeks as I walk over to him. "Baba is my grandmother. She had to go somewhere, but I'm going to bring her home tonight."

"Very mysterious." Benjamin nods. "Where have you been? I've been coming up here every day to look for you, but it's like you and your house just vanished."

"I'm sorry. You must have been so worried about Benji – I mean your lamb. I called him Benji." My cheeks burn. "I didn't want to go, but the house, I mean, *we* had to leave suddenly and—"

"It's all right." Benjamin glances over at Benji. "I knew you'd take care of him. It's you I was worried about…I mean, looking for." His ears blush pink. "It's good to see you again."

"You too." My smile widens. "Would you like to help me build the fence? I know you like the bones."

Benjamin helps me set up the femurs and fibulas, string up vertebrae and balance the skulls on top.

At lunchtime I bring out a bottle of *kvass*, and some of the food I made for the guiding last night that never got eaten. Benjamin spreads out a blanket and I cover it with plates of *pirog*, *vatrushka*, bread and butter, and sweet *pastilas* for dessert.

"I've been wondering what *kvass* tastes like since you left." Benjamin sniffs the drink and takes a sip. "Interesting." He pulls a strange face, like he sucked on a lemon. "It's sour and fizzy. I like it." He smiles and takes a bigger swig. "So where have you been?"

"You wouldn't believe me if I told you." I break a piece off a *pirog* for Jack and take a big bite of the rest.

"Tell me anyway." Benjamin looks at all the food like he doesn't know where to start. He picks up a *pirog* in one hand, a *vatrushka* in the other, and leans back.

"I've been in the desert, watching ant-lion traps and turning cartwheels in the sand. I took a friend to see the ocean for the first time, jumped over waves on a tropical beach and chased an octopus through the shallows. I made some friends in a market, who turned out not to be friends at all, but I saw a snake charmer and swam in a beautiful riad. I made fireworks with—" A lump forms in my throat. I can almost hear the Old Yaga telling me Baba is gone and going through The Gate is not worth the risk.

Benjamin looks at me curiously, like he's trying to figure something out.

"How's school?" I ask, wanting to change the subject. "Still suspended?"

"No, I'm back. And I've stopped having stupid arguments with the boys." Benjamin sighs. "But I still don't fit in there though."

I nod. This time I know what Benjamin means. I don't fit in with the living, the dead or the Yaga.

"School does have a few good bits, I suppose." Benjamin smiles. "There's a new art teacher I like, and in another class we're building bird feeders."

"That sounds fun." I think how nice it would be if I could fill my life with all the best bits of being living, dead and Yaga. If I could make friends, but still live in the house, go to Yaga parties, but not have to hide far from towns. I brush the thoughts away. There's no point daydreaming about a life I can't have.

"How long are you staying this time?" Benjamin asks.

"I don't know." I give the last of my *pirog* to Jack, my heart sinking through my chest. "When Baba comes home, we'll probably move on again."

"That's a shame." Benjamin looks back over at Benji. "Would you like to keep him?"

"Oh, no." I shake my head. "I mean, I'd love to, but he'll be better off with you. We move around so much. He would be happier here." Jack flaps up onto my shoulder and my heart stops as I realize something.

Tonight, like the Old Yaga said, I might not be able to come back through The Gate. I'm dead. I might return to the stars, and Jack would be left all alone.

"Can you keep Jack?" I ask quickly, before I change my mind. "Just for tonight, while I get Baba."

"Of course." Benjamin lifts his elbow and balances a piece of bread on it. Jack eyes it suspiciously and turns away.

"Go on, Jack." I gather him up and place him in Benjamin's arms. "I'll see you tomorrow."

Jack squawks loudly and struggles to flap away. Benjamin offers him the bread again, but Jack snatches it angrily and shoves it in Benjamin's ear.

"Sorry. He does that a lot. You may end up with spiders and beetles in your ears and socks, too."

"I don't mind." Benjamin holds Jack close and strokes his feathers until he calms down. A wave of relief washes over me. If I can't come back, at least I know Benjamin will take care of Jack, and he'll be safe.

The sun dips behind the mountain on the other side of the valley and a cool shadow falls over us. "I need to get ready for tonight." I stand and turn away, blinking back tears. The thought I might not see Jack, Benjamin, Benji or the beautiful view behind me ever again is overwhelming. My body feels wobbly and no matter how much I blink and breathe, I know I won't be able to stop the tears from falling.

I force an image of Baba to the front of my mind and try to convince myself I'm doing the right thing. I need to bring Baba home. It's all I've wanted to do since she left, and finally, tonight, the house is going to let me try.

THROUGH
THE GATE

Fingers trembling, I light the skulls. The lights in the little town by the lake blink on too, throwing an orange glow across the darkness below. I try my best to ignore them, wipe my hands on my apron, and make sure the fence gate is shut tight.

I go into the house, sit at the table and wait, a strange tingling rising up the back of my neck. I stand again, not knowing what to do with myself, and walk around the room.

The house has been healing well. There are few signs now of the damage caused by the fire. Most of the burned wood has grown back, even stronger than before. All the furniture and fabrics are clean, although the odd scorch mark remains. I move into my bedroom and look at the mossy fort the house grew for me and my eyes sting.

"What will happen to you if I don't come back?" I ask the rafters.

The house shrugs its eaves and stretches its legs. I suppose that means it will run off to find another Yaga to bond with. I purse my lips and shake my hair away from my face. I don't want to be the next Guardian, but the thought of someone else in my and Baba's house makes my chest burn.

I stride back into the front room and stare at the space where The Gate will open. "Go on then, open it." I don't mean to say the words so harshly so I add, "Please." All the muscles in my body are tightly coiled, my jaw clenched. I need to do this now, before I change my mind.

A rush of air swishes down the chimney and all the candles flicker out. I blink, adjusting my eyes to the darkness, and see stars in the distance, far away. I step towards The Gate, my legs heavy and a hard knot in my stomach.

The closer I get, the stronger I feel the pull of the

stars, as real as if they were tugging on my skirt with long, cool fingers. My heart drums in my chest and blood surges round my body faster than ever before. It pounds in my ears and I gasp at how alive I feel all of a sudden.

I stand on the last floorboard and lean into The Gate. Fear shivers through me. It feels like I'm on tiptoe at the edge of a great cliff and just a breath of wind would be enough to lift me up and away.

I picture Baba, smiling her crooked-toothed smile and dancing with the dead, and I focus on keeping that image right at the front of my mind as I take one more step.

Silence envelops me as I enter the darkness. Then lights appear, one by one, flickering like fireflies. They're beautiful. They move slowly at first, then they accelerate upwards until they are lines of light and I realize it's me that's moving, not them. I'm falling. My ears pop from the pressure change and immediately I hear the roar of the black ocean below.

Panic speeds my heart until it is thundering against my ribcage. Something is wrong. The dead float

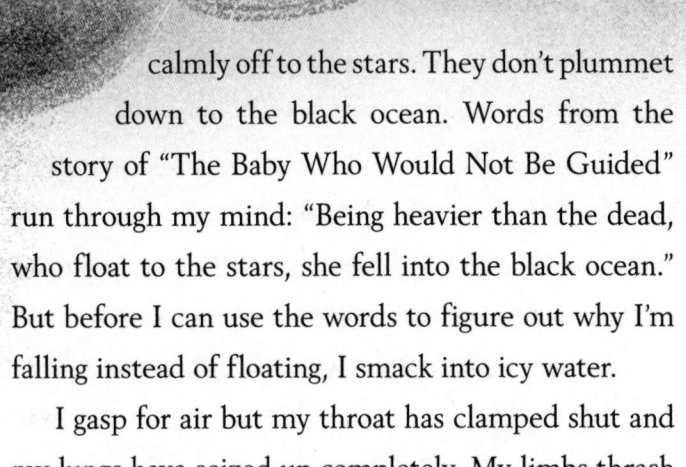

calmly off to the stars. They don't plummet down to the black ocean. Words from the story of "The Baby Who Would Not Be Guided" run through my mind: "Being heavier than the dead, who float to the stars, she fell into the black ocean." But before I can use the words to figure out why I'm falling instead of floating, I smack into icy water.

I gasp for air but my throat has clamped shut and my lungs have seized up completely. My limbs thrash around uselessly as I'm tossed upwards by great waves, and pulled back and forth by freezing currents.

Just as I think my chest will explode, my airways burst open and air rushes in. I breathe and kick my legs rhythmically, counting beats in my mind until I feel in control. Then I start to swim.

In the distance, waves are smashing
onto the glassy mountains with a clinking
that reminds me of walking over Hollow
Stones with Benjamin. I swim towards the noise,
rising and falling over the swell of the waves, until my
whole body is aching and numb from the cold.

Glimpses of light, reflected in the sheer glass cliffs,
run past my eyes. A huge wave lifts me up and throws
me into the hard, flat surface. My hands slide down,
searching for a grip, but it's smooth as a mirror.

No matter how hard I try I can't get a purchase
on the glass. Each time I slip back into the icy water,
my head burns with frustration. I even try to use
my teeth and nails, like Baba in the story, but
it's hopeless. The mountain rises up for ever;

smooth, dark and impossible. What am I going to do? I can't go back, I can't go on...

"Ouch!" Something collides with my shoulder with a deafening squawk and a dramatic ruffle of soaking-wet feathers. "Jack! What are you doing here?" My voice is breathless, overpowered by the crash of freezing waves.

Jack jumps onto the glass and his claws sink in with a crack. He pecks at the surface until a hole widens beneath his beak. When it's deep enough for me to get a few fingers in, he hops up the cliff face and pecks another hole.

I heave myself up. The glass digs painfully into my fingers, but it gets easier when I can push my toes into the holes and use my feet too. The roar of the ocean fades as I climb higher, until it's just a whisper far below. Finally my hands curl around the top of the mountain and I pull myself up onto a small flat peak.

The universe surrounds us, light and colour drifting through inky darkness: silver stars, purple and green nebulae and billowing red clouds. Meteors, or maybe the souls of the dead, fly past on their way back to the stars. I lift my hand to my mouth and stare at the endless space, my eyes aching from opening so wide.

Jack lands on my shoulder and I stroke his neck. I want to tell him off for following me, and thank him for helping, but I don't say anything. Words just aren't enough. We watch as a long, milky path of stars rotates towards us, until its shining light is right at my feet. With a deep breath to fill my lungs with courage, I close my eyes and step onto it, half expecting to fall through it as if it was a cloud.

But my feet float above the path. I open my eyes, smile, and begin the long walk to the stars. It's not cold, nor warm. I can't feel my wet clothes against my body, or the water I see dripping from my hair. But I feel the ache in my legs, getting more intense the further I walk.

I lose all sense of time, and tiredness makes my eyelids heavy. They fall over my eyes and flicker back up when I realize I'm drifting to sleep, until suddenly they open to blazing light ahead. Stars are swirling, like glitter in a whirlpool, the light intensifying to a centre that is too bright to look at.

Jack digs his claws into my shoulder and flaps his wings, as if he's trying to pull me back. But I run towards the light, slowly at first because my legs are so heavy, but I pick up speed as I get closer. This is the birthplace of the stars. This is where I'll find Baba.

The light surrounds me, clinging to my skin like static until I glow with it. I look up at Jack and he's covered with it too, his feathers matching his bright silver eyes. Laughter rises in my throat but is swept away by the currents of light.

"Baba!" I shout. My voice flows into the stars. "Baba!" I yell again, but there's no answer.

My limbs float up and a feeling of weightlessness

relaxes my body. I spin slowly as I'm pulled towards the centre, where the light is brightest. Glittery layers accumulate on my skin. The light whirls around me and Jack, sparkling everywhere I turn. It's warm and peaceful. But I can't feel Baba at all. I felt closer to her at home, in our house, than I do now.

She's not here.

I try to blink away the light and the glitter and the tears, as I realize the truth.

She's not here. Not as I remember her anyway. She's something else now, some part of this swirling light and energy that I don't understand.

I look at my hands and see them fading, dissolving into the light. Suddenly I want to leave, more than anything. I don't want to be a part of this. Not yet. I move my arms and legs, like I'm swimming, and try to go back in the direction I came.

"Marinka!" A voice reverberates through the light, sending tiny sparks flying into curling eddies. It's a boy's voice, far away. I swim towards it as fast as I can.

"Marinka!" he calls again and I recognize him. Benjamin! My feet brush onto the starry path and I run over it, sweeping light and glitter from my arms.

"Benjamin!" I shout, looking back across the endless darkness of space. I think I see his silhouette, a tiny black outline against a distant rectangle of light. The Gate. My house is on the other side. I sprint as fast as I can, light showering around me as Jack flaps it from his wings.

The pull of the stars is behind me. I feel it at my back. But the pull of The Gate, my house and Benjamin is stronger. I know exactly where I want to be.

As I step onto the top of the glassy mountain I look at The Gate, high above the black ocean, and my heart sinks. How can I reach it?

I think about jumping. I'm dead after all; I'm meant to float and drift here. But last time I just fell into the water. If I do that again, I'll never get up to The Gate.

There must be a way. Baba must have done this too. I try to remember all the words of "The Baby Who Would Not Be Guided". Did Baba ride a solar wind or a meteor shower, or drift on the back of a storm cloud? Nothing makes sense.

"What can I do, Jack?" My forehead tenses as I try desperately to think of a plan.

Jack squawks and flaps off my shoulder towards The Gate. I stare at the space he disappeared into, unblinking, until my eyes burn. Finally I hear his cry, and see his dark outline hurtling towards me. He has something in his mouth. A smile bursts across my face as I realize what it is.

He circles, wrapping the vine around my waist. I loop it round a few more times, pull it tight and tie a knot. Straight away I feel the house tugging the other end. I close my eyes and step off the cliff.

Just as before, my fall starts slowly. It's like the darkness is weighing me up, deciding whether to drop me or carry me. Then it lets go and I plummet downwards. Only this time the vine catches me, yanking sharply at my waist, and I'm left dangling over the rolling, crashing waves.

The vine rises, pulling me towards The Gate and my house. I twist my body round and grip the vine tight and, hand over hand, I climb. When the rectangle of light is right above me I look up to see Benjamin smiling down. He reaches out and offers me his hands.

Even though I could climb the last bit myself, I wrap my fingers around Benjamin's and beam as he pulls me into the house. I roll onto the floorboards and smell *kvass*, *borsch* and the wet feathers of Jack beside me. The Gate blinks shut and the vine round my waist unfurls and flows back up to the rafter it grew from.

310

"Thank you," I murmur to the house, Jack and Benjamin.

"What was that?" Benjamin stares at the space where The Gate was.

"I'm not supposed to say." I sit up, shivering, suddenly intensely aware of the cold wet clothes against my skin.

Benjamin pulls my horsehair blanket from Baba's chair and wraps it around me. "It doesn't look like the sort of place you'd want to go."

"No," I agree. "Not yet anyway, but I was looking for my grandmother."

"Did you find her?"

I shake my head, blinking back tears. "She's gone." The words nearly choke me. I take a deep breath, trying to loosen the tightness crushing my chest.

"I'm sorry." Benjamin helps me into Baba's chair and hangs the kettle over the fire. The warmth of the flames wraps around me and blood tingles into my fingers.

"What are you doing here?" I ask.

"Your house came and got me." Benjamin smiles.

"Seems you weren't joking when you said it could walk."

I glance up at the rafters in disbelief. I can't believe the house actually went and got Benjamin, a living person, to help me come home. I pat the mantelpiece gratefully. "Thank you, House."

"It was a bit of a shock." Benjamin sits opposite me. "I was sketching the birds singing the dawn chorus in the field behind my house and these huge footsteps came thumping towards me. I looked up and saw your house, running." Benjamin laughs. "It scared the life out of me, and the birds I was drawing. They all flew away in different directions. One of them flew right into my head. Then the door to your house opened, all by itself, and I came in looking for you." Benjamin's ears flush pink. "And I guess you know the rest."

I look out of the window, curious to see where we are. Soft dawn light illuminates dewdrops on a grassy field. A few houses are nestled together on the other side. The gardens between them are filled with colourful flowers and small birds flutter between feeders, chirping happily.

"We're in the valley? In your village?" Tears creep from the corners of my eyes, though I'm not sure why. Maybe it's because the house has never settled so close to the homes of the living before. Maybe it's because it has done this for me.

Benjamin makes cocoa and we take it outside and sit on the porch steps, sipping our drinks and eating the last of the spiced honey bread. I break off chunks and feed them to Jack and he brings me worms he keeps digging out from the soft wet earth.

"Jack must have found a way out of my room as soon as I fell asleep." Benjamin shakes his head. "I'm sorry."

"Don't be. I'm glad he did." I lift my elbow and Jack hops onto it for a stroke.

"How long will you and Jack and your house stay in the village?" Benjamin asks.

"I don't know," I confess. "That's up to the house." A chill runs through me as I remember the crack by the skeleton store.

The walls of the house creak and it rocks slightly, burying itself deeper into the ground as if it wants to show me how comfortable it is here and tell me that the crack is a problem for another day. My heart does a little flip as I realize we're going to stay for a while.

Baba used to say it's not how long a life, but how sweet a life that counts, and I think maybe the same is true with friendships. I'm not sure how long I will get to spend with Benjamin, but I will appreciate the time I have. I wish I had appreciated the moments I had with Baba more. Nobody is yours to keep. Nothing is for ever.

"What are you going to do today?" Benjamin puts down his mug and stretches his arms up to the sky.

"I don't know." I pull my horsehair blanket tight around me and glance at the skeleton store, but the door to it stays firmly shut so I know the house doesn't want me to guide tonight. An empty feeling swells inside me and I frown. With no fence to build, no guiding to prepare for, and no Baba to welcome home, what do I do?

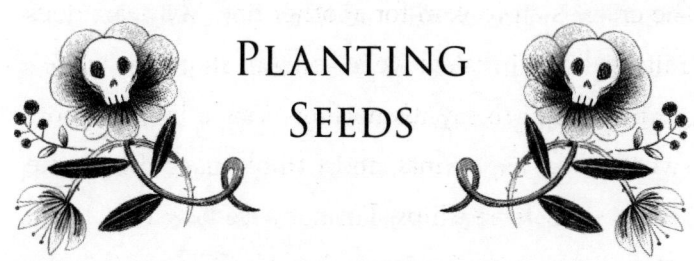

Planting
Seeds

Benjamin sits on the porch sketching Jack, while I change into clean dry clothes. Then he insists I come to his house for a meal. It's just the other side of the field, so I know I won't fade, but I can't help checking my hands as I walk across the grass anyway.

Benjamin's father is nice. He shakes my hand and tells me Benjamin has told him all about me. Then he makes us tea, and we sit drinking it in a warm kitchen while he cooks for us all. Benjamin shows his father my house through the window and tells him I'm here on holiday. His father stares at my house, stroking his chin in confusion.

"But how did it get here?" he asks finally.

"It walked." Benjamin winks at me and I smile.

I love the roasted potatoes, garden peas, small round herby breads and puddings, but I politely refuse the grilled lamb, my gaze drifting to Benji, who is frolicking outside the window.

"Are you keeping Benji as a pet?" I ask, shuddering at the thought that Benjamin's father may have plans to eat him.

"Yes, he's safe from my plate." Benjamin's father nods quickly as he realizes what I'm thinking. "That field is part of our garden. He can graze there and live to a ripe old age."

"I didn't know it was your field." Heat rises into my cheeks as I realize the house has settled in their garden, "I'm sorry about the house—"

"It's fine," Benjamin's father rushes in. "You can stay there as long as you like, we don't use it for much. There are just a few growing beds around the edges. Would you like to see them?"

The afternoon whizzes past. Benjamin and his father show me the freshly turned earth of their vegetable patch, surrounded by potted shrubs and herbs. Insects dance over a small wild flower meadow, and a tangled row of bushes is alive with birds.

Nina would love this place. Thinking of her brings a rush of sadness, but then Benjamin opens a box full of seeds and asks if I would like to plant some. Right on the top is a packet of oleander seeds, like the ones Nina said her father planted for her mother.

I pick them up with trembling fingers and my breath catches in my throat when I see the packet beneath them. It has a picture of a flower on it: a tiny star-shaped pink-and-white flower, like the one Baba gave me in the desert when she hugged me and called me her *pchelka*.

It feels like a sign that Baba and Nina have forgiven me, and that everything is going to be all right. We plant the seeds in tiny pots and Benjamin gives me two of each to take home and grow on my porch.

When dusk falls, Benjamin and his father walk me back to my house. I do want to go home, but the thought of being alone all night, with only Jack for company, gives me a heavy sinking feeling.

As we draw close, the house narrows its windows, as if peering into the darkness to see who I'm with.

Then, without warning, it stands up, takes a big step forward and sits down again, right in front of us.

Benjamin's father freezes mid-step. His jaw drops open and he makes a kind of gasping sound. "W...wh?" he stammers, and looks from the house, to me, to Benjamin.

Benjamin shrugs. "I told you it walked."

We help Benjamin's father into the house and sit him in front of the fire. Pale and cold with shock, he doesn't speak again until he's warmed up with a hot drink. Then he asks question after question.

There's not much I can say other than the house has legs, is alive, and takes care of me. I tell Benjamin's father that by showing its legs, the house is trusting him and Benjamin with a big secret. Benjamin's father says he understands the importance of this, and even makes up a story about me being Benjamin's cousin to tell the other villagers. But when he realizes I'm living in the house by myself he doesn't want to leave me on my own. It takes a while to convince him I'll be fine. Finally he agrees to go when I promise to come over for breakfast in the morning.

I sit on the porch steps after they've left, staring up at the stars and the moon peeking out from behind a white wispy cloud. Baba is somewhere out there, and she isn't coming home.

I'll never see her again, never watch her smiling and dancing with the dead, never hear her play music, never be pulled into one of her hugs, or lean against her as she tells me a story. An intense wave of grief suffocates me, trapping a scream inside my chest. Every muscle in my body shudders and tears pour down my tight, screwed-up face.

The house sways gently, as if it wants to rock me to sleep. I feel the balustrade wrap around my shoulders in a stiff wooden hug and the spindles pat me gently. I entwine my arms through the balustrade, and hug the house back.

A painful creak sounds in the distance, followed by a crack and a thump, then another creak. "What is that?" I ask, squinting into the darkness. Jack flaps off the roof towards the noise. He returns a few minutes later, circling in the air and squawking excitedly.

Creak. Crack. Thump. Creak. Crack. Thump. The noises escalate as whatever it is draws closer. A huge dark shadow emerges and collapses with a bang and a clatter right next to my house. The door swings open and the Old Yaga steps out with a smile.

"Greetings, Yaga Marinka. I'm very pleased to see you."

"Your house!" I stare at her broken, crumpled house. Its legs are cracked, its roof and windows sagging.

"It's been a long walk. There were a few times I didn't think we'd make it." The Old Yaga looks up at her house with a mixture of sadness and pride. "You did well." She pats the balustrade, steps off her porch and strides towards me.

"Why did you come here? How did you know where I was?" The thought of her house struggling all the way here and arriving in this state, just so the Old Yaga could see me, makes me burn with guilt.

"I hear the whispers through The Gates, remember?" She sits down on the step next to me and smiles. "And I heard a pretty big splash when you fell into the black ocean."

I look away, blood rushing into my cheeks.

"Oh, don't worry." The Old Yaga waves my guilt and shame away. "Some mistakes you have to make for yourself. I'm just glad you got home safe. It's that splash that interests me."

"Why?" I look at her in confusion.

She leans towards me, her eyes sparkling. "The dead float to the stars. Only the living make a splash."

Breath flutters into my chest and I feel it in an entirely new and different way; as cool air rushing into real, live lungs. But that's not possible. Is it?

GROWING

I stare at the Old Yaga in shock. "What are you saying?" I whisper, electricity rushing over my skin.

"Well, I don't know for sure." The Old Yaga leans back against the porch steps. "But I think your house might have worked a bit of Yaga magic."

The house puffs itself up behind me.

"I don't understand." The back of my neck tingles. I don't want to jump to conclusions, or raise my hopes just to have them smashed to pieces.

"Yaga houses give the dead energy so they can seem alive."

I nod slowly.

"So maybe your house has given you energy to actually be alive. For real."

"Is that even possible?" I ask, hardly daring to believe it.

"I don't see why not. I've thought about this a lot on the way here, and I can't think of another reason you would fall into the black ocean. Perhaps your house made you alive before you went through The Gate in an effort to stop you returning to the stars. Or maybe your house simply decided the best way to make you happy was to make you alive." The Old Yaga glances from her house to mine. "Yaga houses are clever and loyal. If they know what their Yaga wants, they'll do everything they can to give it to them. Like my house grew me a laboratory, and walked me all the way here." She gazes at her house affectionately, then turns back to me. "I think your house made you alive because it wants you to be happy."

"Is this true?" I ask the nearest window, more aware than ever before of the blood rushing through my veins. "Am I alive?"

The house nods and shrugs at the same time. Like it's not quite sure whether its efforts to make me alive have worked.

"How can I find out for certain?" I look from the house to the Old Yaga.

"Perhaps in the morning you can walk to that town by the lake, to see if you fade," the Old Yaga suggests with a smile.

"I can't wait till morning." I shake my head, buzzing with excitement. "I'll never be able to sleep."

"Of course you will." The Old Yaga ushers me into my house. "You've had a busy time lately, and you've a busy day ahead tomorrow. You need your sleep. Especially if you are alive."

I get ready for bed, experiencing every sensation as if it were for the first time: the water splashing onto my skin when I wash my face, the fresh scent of the pine soap, the warmth radiating from my body and becoming trapped under my blankets, the softness of Jack's feathers as I kiss him goodnight, and the whisper of night-time breezes through the grassy field. I don't know if I'm imagining how different everything seems, or if it's because I really am alive.

As I'm falling asleep, a dark thought creeps into my mind. If I am alive, what does that mean for me and the house? Will it leave me now? A Yaga house needs a Guardian to guide the dead. Not a living girl who wants a life with the living.

I frown and a tight pain squeezes my chest. I've lived in a Yaga house all my life, with a Yaga grandmother. Which makes me Yaga too. I don't want to lose the house to be with the living, because I'm not quite like them. And because I need my house.

My thoughts seep into my dreams, and they end up being filled with uncomfortable visions of living in a house that can't grow you mossy forts, or play hide-and-seek with you, or chase you till you're breathless, or hug you on its porch.

I'm woken by voices, but my head is so foggy it takes me a moment to recognize who they belong to: the Old Yaga, Benjamin and his father. They're all outside, talking and laughing like old friends. I wander out to join them, rubbing the sleep from my eyes.

"Good morning, Marinka." The Old Yaga passes me

a mug of tea. "You're just in time, it should still be warm."

"Thank you." I sit on the porch steps and smile a greeting to Benjamin and his father. "So you've met Tatyana." I only just remember not to call her the Old Yaga, or Yaga Tatyana.

"Yes." Benjamin's father nods. "Tatyana says she's an old friend of your grandmother's. I'm so pleased she's here to keep an eye on you. I must admit I was worried when you said you were living alone. That's why we came over when you didn't show up for breakfast this morning."

I look up at the sky and realize it's nearly the middle of the day. "Sorry, I must have overslept."

"It doesn't matter." Benjamin smiles. "Do you fancy coming into town? There's a music festival by the lake. We could walk there together."

My muscles tense, filling with nervous excitement. I glance at the Old Yaga and she beams back at me. "I'll make you some *kasha* while you get ready," she offers. "Then you could meet Benjamin at his house."

When I'm ready to go, I stand on the last step of the porch, palms sweating, legs like lead.

"You'll be fine." The Old Yaga nudges me onto the grass.

"What if I fade?" My heart dips at the thought.

"Tell Benjamin you don't feel well, and come home."

I take a deep breath and turn to wave at my house, but it's the Old Yaga's house that catches my eye. The damage looks even worse than last night. Her whole house seems to be falling apart and sinking into the ground. "Is your house going to be all right?" I ask, my forehead crumpling.

The Old Yaga's eyes get damp and shiny. She opens her mouth, but no words come out. Before I know what I'm doing, I wrap my arms around her and squeeze. She squeezes back, a small laugh escaping from her throat. "Go on," she says. "I'm just being silly. You go and have some fun." She squeezes me once more, then gently pushes me away and walks back to her house. "I'll spend some time with my house, and see you when you get back." She raises her hand and disappears through her front door.

I turn to my house. "House," I whisper, "is there anything you can do to help the Old Yaga's house?"

The door frame purses together and the windows narrow.

"If it's true, about you doing what you can to make me happy – and I know you've done lots already, maybe even made me alive when you didn't have to…" I take a trembling breath. "I might be asking too much, but if there *is* anything you can do to save her house, then…" I'm not sure what else to say. "Please?"

The house gives a little nod, and I smile.

I walk to Benjamin's house with a spring in my step. And my cheeks ache from smiling as we wander away from the village, towards the little town by the lake.

Although I keep checking my hands to see if they'll fade, I know in my heart they won't. I feel too alive to be dead. Blood rushes through my veins, and my mind buzzes with all the new things I see and hear and touch.

We follow a path along the lake shore. Light and shadows dance beneath a canopy of rustling leaves. Cormorants rest on tiny islands, their wings held open to dry. Geese honk warnings to stay away from their nests in the reeds, as fluffy goslings wobble around at their feet.

The lake laps gently onto the shore, reflecting the mountains and the sky and soft white clouds that remind me of Baba's hair. I dip my fingers into the cool water and pick up smooth, shining stones.

Before I know it we are skirting the edge of the town, walking past market stalls and buildings and real, live, living people. I feel almost as weightless as I did in the stars. My gaze flits from shop windows filled with food, to people holding hands and wearing friendly smiles. Everyone is getting on with their day like it is so ordinary, while inside I am bursting with the wonder of it all.

The festival is in a park that runs from the edge of the town to the shore of the lake. A stage has been set up and a huge group of drummers are on it, sending beats thrumming into the air. Every muscle in my body vibrates, and it must be the same for all the other people, because they are bouncing around everywhere, like me.

Different musicians take turns on the stage; some dance with instruments that shine in the sun, and others strum guitars and sing. Melodies rise up and drift across the lake. Baba would have loved all this music so much. Thinking of her makes my body feel heavy and the bounce in my feet disappears.

Benjamin must notice because he asks if I want to rest, and get something to eat from one of the food stalls. I choose something that looks like a pink fluffy cloud, because I can't possibly imagine what it might taste like. I break off sticky wisps and let them dissolve on my tongue, while Benjamin pulls off chunks and squashes them until they look like solid pink sweets.

The sun sets but the music plays on. We dance some more in front of the stage, surrounded by living people, until I feel like there is no air left in my lungs. Finally the festival ends and we wander back along the lake shore, watching silver moonbeams curl over ripples.

Both my mind and body are heavy and tired, but it's one of the nicest, warmest feelings I've ever had, because I'm worn out from doing some of the things

I've only ever dreamed of. I'm bursting to get home and tell the house and the Old Yaga about my day.

"Can you wait a moment?" Benjamin asks when we reach his house. "I've got something for you."

He runs inside and comes out with a frame that looks familiar. It's the photograph of Baba and me, from when I was a baby. His ears blush pink. "I borrowed this without asking and I'm sorry, but there was a good reason." He passes me a large piece of paper with his other hand.

It's the sketch he drew of me and Jack in the bothy, but he's added Baba to the picture. She looks just like she does in the photograph he borrowed, a huge smile and eyes filled with pride. He's changed the drawing of me and Jack a little too, added more shading and detail, and when I look at my eyes in the picture they seem happier than in the original, a twinkle of excitement shining in each of my pupils.

"I hope you don't mind." Benjamin shuffles his feet nervously.

"I love it," I whisper. "It's perfect."

The moon is big and bright above me as I wander

back across the field to my house. Its silhouette looks different somehow and I tilt my head to try and figure out what's going on.

A new section of floor is extending out from one side of the porch, and two new walls are rising up either side. Three shoots, which will probably thicken into roof joists, are growing between the walls. As I draw closer, I realize the new room is connecting the two houses.

Vines are clambering across the walls and creeping over the Old Yaga's house. Even in the darkness I can see her house is healing where the vines are touching it. The wooden walls are stronger, more upright, and gleaming in the moonlight like they have been polished with beeswax.

I step up onto the soft new floor and notice the Old Yaga sitting in the middle, watching fresh shoots emerge from the top of the walls and weave their way across the space above us. Jack is on her shoulder but he squawks when he sees me and flaps over to my elbow.

The Old Yaga looks up at me and smiles, but she

doesn't say anything. I sit next to her, in silence under the stars, and we watch as our houses grow together through the night.

YAGA AND MORE THAN YAGA

My house has chicken legs, but most of the year it is settled in a small village near a twinkling town that curves around the edge of a lake. My friend Benjamin lives across the field and the lamb Benji roams in the grass and wild flowers between us.

He's a fat hungry sheep now. Baba would have loved him in a mutton *borsch*. I still miss Baba, but she's always here, in my thoughts, whenever I need her, and I have Jack for company and my house takes good care of me.

The Old Yaga watches over me too. Our houses have grown together into one. The Old Yaga's house's legs seized up and grew back into the floorboards, but my house's legs have grown thicker, stronger and wider spaced to cope with the extra weight. If anything, my house runs faster now. There wasn't another house that could beat it when we raced across The Steppes in the summer.

I am living, dead, and Yaga. Different to everyone I meet. But I am happy this way. It means I can move between different worlds.

Yaga love to visit us, to talk about my death, my life and the journeys I've made to the stars. They buy spirit *trost* from the Old Yaga, share their own stories with us and collect copies of the *Yaga Tales*, which I am helping the Old Yaga to write and press more often.

I have a life with the living too. I go to the little town by the lake; use the library, watch shows in the theatre, and Benjamin's father has even arranged for me to try school a couple of days a week.

My destiny is undecided, and that's how I like it. The possibilities are as endless as the stars. They fill the living world and the Yaga world, and they even twinkle in the parties for the dead.

I help the Old Yaga with the guidings, and sometimes I even guide a few souls myself. It turns out guiding isn't so bad when you have a life of your own, too.

We never guide in The Land of Lakes, though. While we're here the house keeps the skeleton store firmly shut. But whenever the urge takes it, the house stands up in the middle of the night and carries me and the Old Yaga, and sometimes Benjamin and his father, somewhere new. I love the fact our house has legs. We can go anywhere together.

We travel to islands and wetlands, rainforests and heathlands, high mountains and deep ravines. When we arrive we build the fence, light the skull candles and prepare a feast. The parties are always good. We sing and dance with the dead, listen to their stories and then guide them through The Gate.

The best parties are Yaga parties though. The Old Yaga and Yaga Onekin have been working on a plan to get the Yaga houses together at least once a season. So far they've arranged the race on The Steppes, and a square dance in The Land of Tall Trees. Soon we're having a starlit swim on the beach of a small, uninhabited, tropical island.

But at this moment our house is sitting in Benjamin's father's field. I'm on the porch steps, watching a family of deer graze in the moonlight. The Old Yaga sits next to me, puffs on her pipe and the smoke drifts up to the stars.

Jack struts around below the last step, picking at the ground, searching for worms. It rained earlier so the earth is soft and wet. The Old Yaga points her pipe to a puddle near Jack's feet. "What do you see?" she asks.

I lean forward and peer into the water, expecting to see my reflection; my red hair curling out from under my new woollen hat. Jack flings a small stone into the air and it lands in the puddle, sending ripples rolling across the surface. The sky dances in the water, the silver moon and the firefly stars and the endless arc of the Milky Way. I see the whole universe in the tiny puddle and I smile.

Marinka's glossary

Balalaika: a musical instrument with a triangular body and three strings

Beghrir: a spongy pancake soaked in honey

Bessara: a thick bean soup

Blini: small pancakes

Borsch: beetroot soup; there are many different varieties to suit different tastes

Chak-chak: deep-fried balls of dough, drenched in hot honey and left to harden

Circassian cheese: a mild, soft cheese

Kasha: porridge, often made from buckwheat

Kissel: a dessert made from thickened fruit juice

Kolbasa: a type of boiled or smoked sausage

Kozinaki: a sweet bar made from nuts, seeds, and honey

Kvass: a sour, tangy drink made by fermenting bread or grains

Magaria: a desert tree with brown, cherry-sized fruits

Pastilas: bars of baked jellied fruit

Pchelka: little bee, a term of endearment

Pirog: a pie with a sweet or savoury filling

Shchi: cabbage soup

Shebakia: a deep-fried sesame cookie coated in honey

Trost (spirit *trost*): the fiery drink for the dead; named *trost* after a walking stick, because it helps them on their journey

Tushonka: tinned stewed meat

Ukha: fish broth

Vatrushka: a round pastry usually filled with cheese

Vobla: a type of fish

Zakusi: snacks usually eaten before a meal

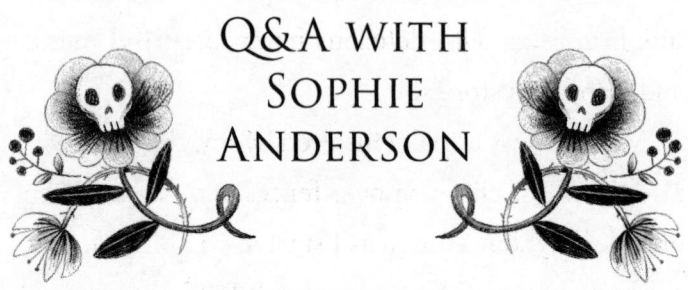

Q&A WITH SOPHIE ANDERSON

Sophie, tell us a little bit about what inspired The House with Chicken Legs?

My grandmother told me fairy tales about Baba Yaga and her house with chicken legs when I was young. Some of the stories were terrifying, but they fascinated me too. Baba Yaga is much more than your average fairy-tale witch. She can be cruel, but also kind and compassionate. I wanted to explore this side of Baba Yaga, while giving her a role that explained people's fear of her, and her links with death.

The house in *The House with Chicken Legs* ended up being similar to my grandmother's home: filled

with memories of the dead, but also a celebration of life; brimming with delicious foods, beautiful music, and wondrous stories.

Marinka was initially inspired by my children, who also dream of climbing over fences and carving their own destiny. But as soon as I started writing Marinka, she became incredibly real to me. It felt like her world and her story already existed, and I had simply discovered a window into it.

What are your favourite myths or folk stories?

Slavic fairy tales have a special place in my heart, because of my grandmother. My favourites include *Vasilisa the Beautiful*, who completes seemingly impossible tasks set by Baba Yaga to earn a skull with burning eyes that frees her from her evil stepmother; *The Snow Maiden*, who sought out love and happiness even though it made her melt; and *Sadko*, who played music until The Tsar of the Sea danced up a storm.

I also love folk stories from all over the world; African tales about *Anansi*, a wise and cunning spider-man

who spun a web to the sky to ask for the Sky God's stories; African-American tales of *Brer Rabbit*, who uses intelligence to prevail over larger animals; and the Middle Eastern stories from *One Thousand and One Nights*, told by Scheherazade to save her life, which include tales of epic journeys, djinn, sorcerers, talking animals and magical objects.

If you had a house with chicken legs for a day, where would you go, or what would you do and why?

I have always wanted to see the places that inspired my grandmother's stories. So, I would sit on the house's roof as it ran over the fells near my current home and the Welsh hills of my childhood, splashed through the English Channel, and galloped all the way across Europe to the enchanted forests, lakes and seas of my grandmother's first home.

But I wouldn't stop there! There is so much of the world I would love to see; northern lights and narwhals, baobabs and bears, snow monkeys soaking in hot springs and migrating monarch butterflies.

The house and I would samba in the streets of Rio, fire dance in Fiji, dip into the Dead Sea, and amble under avenues of cherry blossoms in Korea. I'm not sure I could do all that in one day, but it would be fun to try, and it would certainly inspire some new stories!

What research did you do when you were writing the book?

I read flocks of Slavic fairy tales, including all the Baba Yaga stories I could find. I also researched ancient Slavic beliefs, and many of the ideas I came across – death as a journey, the glassy mountains, the black ocean, and Baba Yaga's links to an ancient Goddess of Death – became incorporated into *The House with Chicken Legs*.

I experimented with Russian recipes, made my first *borsch* and ate my first horseradish. I listened to traditional Russian music, discovered many curious and wonderful Russian proverbs, and visited beautiful places – Venice, Africa, Russia, and the Arctic – from my armchair through the magic of books and film.

The story deals with both dark and light themes – what messages would you like readers to take away from the book?

That life is full of joy and sorrow, loneliness and companionship, pride and regret. To live means experiencing it all. Some things might feel heartbreaking, but they can never truly break your heart. There is always hope for a brighter future, and you might find it in the most unexpected of places – in an encounter with a young friend or an old Yaga, in a house that you thought was your enemy, in the beak of a bird, or in the ripples on a puddle's surface. Even death can inspire us to embrace life.

I hope my readers try to appreciate every moment – whether light or dark – and keep striving for happiness. We can shape and mould our futures, and the possibilities are as endless as the stars!

Can you give us a sneak peek of what's coming next from you, Sophie?

My next book is also inspired by Slavic folklore, especially by a tale called *The Lime Tree* or *Why Bears' Paws are Like Hands*; and, like *The House with Chicken Legs*, it has themes of identity and belonging. The book is set in the Siberian Snow Forest – the largest forest on Earth – and in addition to the human characters there is a courageous weasel, a slightly grumpy wolf, a fearful elk, and a bear or two.

There are several short stories within the main story, inspired by folklore characters such as Zmey Gorynych, Koschei the Deathless and Father Frost. A minor character from *The House with Chicken Legs* appears with a larger role. I wonder if readers can guess who it might be?

Acknowledgements

The House with Chicken Legs has been on a long and wonderful journey, guided by a constellation of literary stars. A universe of gratitude goes out to:

Yaga Gemma Cooper, my agent, who lifted Marinka off the back of an easterly breeze, spooned wisdom into her pages, and sent her (and me) out into the world with a far more hopeful future.

Yaga Rebecca Hill at Usborne and Yaga Mallory Kass at Scholastic, my editors, who welcomed Marinka with open arms, and nurtured her story with passion and insight until it sang more strongly than I ever could have imagined.

The orchestra of kind and talented publishing Yaga who gave Marinka the strength to swim the black ocean and climb the glassy mountains. My thanks to each and every one of you, with an extra strum on the balalaika for Becky Walker, Sarah Stewart, Sarah Cronin, Anna Howorth, Stevie Hopwood and Hannah

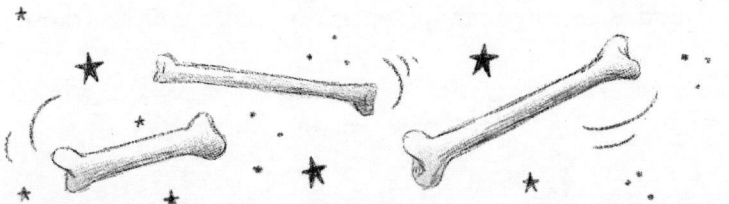

Reardon Steward at Usborne; freelance publicist Fritha Lindqvist; Melissa Schirmer and Maeve Norton at Scholastic; and Giordano Aterini at Rizzoli Ragazzi, whose beautiful letter made me cry (in a good way).

The glittering artists who brought *The House with Chicken Legs* to life in ways more magnificent than I dreamed possible: Katharine Millichope, who designed the perfect cover; Melissa Castrillón, whose gorgeous illustrations adorn the cover; Elisa Paganelli, who enchanted the internal pages with exquisite fairy-tale illustrations; and Red Nose Studios, who rendered *The House with Chicken Legs* from magic and clay for the US cover.

For taking care of my soul while my mind wandered in a house with chicken legs, my infinite love and appreciation belongs to:

My husband Nick and our children Nicky, Alec and Sammy. You make my universe glow and burst with wonder.

The galaxy of family I have on both sides of The Gate: my parents Karen and John, my brothers Ralph and Ross; my grandparents, especially Gerda, whose stories inspired this story; and the family I have been gifted through Nick, with a special toast to Sheila and Frank, for their boundless love and kindness.

My friends: Lorraine, whose laugh lights up the sky; Gillian, who anchors me from the other side of the world; Matthew, who brings me music; and Nadia, who has held my hand from the very first word. And thanks to Ken for the pen, Michelle for the enchanted spinning wheel, and Kiran Millwood Hargrave for the truly magical quote.

A nebula of gratefulness blows to the bibliophiles who help put books into readers' hands: the librarians, teachers, booksellers, reviewers and book bloggers (with an extra gust of thanks to Jo Clarke, Fiona Noble, Vincent Ripley, Scott Evans and Ashley Booth).

And above all, thanks to the readers who spend their precious time with these words and whose imaginations make stories come alive. When a book finds a reader the possibilities are as endless as the stars.

Praise for
The House with Chicken Legs

"I absolutely adored the adventure, love, friendship and stubbornness of Marinka." *Steph, A Little But A Lot*

"A glistening gem of a story with an air of elegance, beauty and fragility." *Scott Evans, The Reader Teacher*

"This book is brimming with real magic and wonder and beauty and heart…" *Stephanie Burgis, author of* The Dragon with a Chocolate Heart

"*The House With Chicken Legs* is the best book I have read in ages. I love the way every chapter leaves you in suspense… I hope Sophie Anderson writes a hundred more books." *Zainab, aged eleven, St Silas CE Primary School*

"A gem of a book with real heart and soul… I love that it doesn't shy away from ideas about bereavement and loneliness, but is comforting and inspiring and hopeful." *Liz Flanagan, author of* Eden Summer

"What a spectacular debut! It oozes with magic and charm… This has all the markings of an MG classic." *Imogen White, author of* The Rose Muddle Mysteries

"A beautiful take on a classic Russian folk tale." *Chicken and Frog bookshop, Brentwood*